Retribution

&

Revenge

Retribution & Revenge

Copyright ©2017 by James E. Bassham All rights reserved

ISBN: 13: 978-1978087002

ISBN: 10: 1978087004

First Print Edition: October 2017

Publisher: Createspace.com

Editor: James E. Bassham

No portion of this publication may be reproduced, stored in any electronic system, transmitted in any form or by any means, electronic, mechanical, photocopy, recording, or otherwise, without written permission from the author.

Events, locales, and conversations have been recreated from memories. In some instances, to maintain anonymity, names of individuals and places have been changed. Some identifying characteristics and details such as physical properties, occupations, and places of residence have been changed. The names, places, and/or people are fictitious. Any that seem real are created from the imagination of the author.

The names of cities, towns, and characters are also a fictitious form of writing.

This book is dedicated to 7 of my closest cousins:

Jackie D. Hancox

Sonya D. Echols

Crystal L. Scott

Angela M. Parker

Leteia "Teia Teia" Claybrooks

Ashley N. Crisp

Lindsay E. Bassham

I'd also like to give a special thanks to my baby sister: **Alethia M. Bassham**, who, after reading the initial draft of "Fresh Out Tha Pen," recommended that I either add more to it, or write a sequel. Well, since you're reading this, it's obvious that I decided to write a sequel.

Acknowledgements, and credit goes, once again, to the creator of the covers of all my books to date: **Author Tamikio L. Reardon**.
Thank you for your patience and guidance, in assisting me through this journey, in this fairly new and exciting world of authorship!

PROLOGUE

It has now been nearly eleven months since Derrick "D-Mac" Franklin was released from South Central Correctional Center. It has been nine months since he was joined in holy matrimony to Rayne Morgan.

After settling into their new home, and investing in numerous real estate properties, which netted abundance in profitable returns, D-Mac finally decided that the time had come to introduce Rayne to his fathers' side of the family, who were in Tennessee's Music City: Nashville.

Saturday, April 11, 2009

"C'mon Rayne!" D-Mac called out. "We gon' be late!"

"I'm coming! I'm coming!" she responded. "Hold your horses!"

It was Rayne's twenty-second birthday, which also happened to be the first birthday she had spent with D-Mac, since his release from prison.

It had been nine months since, with no major complications, which couldn't be handled. But, unknown to Rayne. D-Mac had been unusually busy the previous couple of weeks.

"So, where are we headed?" she inquired.

"Just be cool, sit back, and enjoy the ride!" he smiled.

The first stop they made was the Exxon TigerMarket on Poplar at Highland. After filling the tank of his Lexus LS460L, he jumped on I-40 East, and headed towards Nashville.

When Rayne took notice that they were following the Nashville signs and leaving Memphis, she spoke up.

"What are we going to Nashville for?" she asked.

"You'll see when we get there."

Unbeknownst to Rayne, was the fact that D-Mac also had family in Nashville, among other places. He decided to introduce her to them on her birthday, since she was now a part of the family.

Two hundred miles and two and a half hours later, they were pulling into the Nashville city limits. D-Mac glanced over at Rayne, who had fallen asleep.

"Princess," he called softly. "Princess, we're here."

She slowly opened her eyes and looked around.

"First time in tha 'Ville?" he asked.

"Yeah. But it's nothing like I expected." She admitted.

"Lemme guess. You was expectin' a lotta farmland, barns and horse pastures." D-Mac laughed.

"Yeah. Something like that."

Their first stop was at the Exxon TigerMarket on Trinity Lane at Brick Church Pike.

"You want anything outta here?" he asked.

"Just bring me a Sprite, some Flamin' Hot Cheetos and a Hot Dill Pickle." Rayne responded, with a smile.

D-Mac purchased the items, along with a few items for himself, and paid for the gas.

After filling up the tank, they headed out, once again.

"First, there's someone I want you to meet."

"And who is that?"

They pulled into a gravel driveway on Old Hickory Boulevard in the Madison area.

"This is Derrick Thomas' house." D-Mac announced.

"And he is?"

"My father."

With that, they stepped from the car, approached the front door, and rang the doorbell.

"Hey baby! Come on in!"

It was D-Mac's step-mother, Denise. She invited them in, and hugged them both.

"I knew you was coming, but I wasn't expecting you this early." She said with a smile.

D-Mac made the formal introductions.

"Baby, this is my Nashville mom, Mrs. Thomas. Mom, this is my wife, and your daughter-in-law, Rayne."

"It's good to meet you." Rayne offered.

"Likewise!" Mrs. Thomas replied. "Your dad is still at work, but Candace is downstairs. Twinn and Redd should be over here in a few, when they find out that you're in town. Ellen said that you was gonna go over to her house later."

D-Mac took Rayne downstairs to the basement, where they found his sister, Candace, playing around in the home studio.

"You don' stepped yo skills up, ain't 'cha?" D-Mac called out.

When Candace turned around and saw him, she nearly knocked him over, when she ran up and hugged him.

"Man! You been out almost a year, and y'all just now comin' to see me?" she teased, after hugging Rayne.

"You know me. I've been busy puttin' shit together and stackin' my paper."

The three of them sat down to do a little catching up.

"So, what you been doin' since you been out?" Candace asked.

"Doin' tha same thang I was doin' before I went in." He replied. "Spendin' money tryna make money."

"What you don' bought now?"

"I spent nearly $900,000 on three houses." He began. "Then, four months ago, I bought two more for $650,000."

"Damn!" Candace interrupted. "I need to move down there wit you!"

"You can if you want to." He offered. "I'm rentin' out four of tha houses, but we live in tha biggest of tha five.

"How big is it?"

"Four bedrooms, three and a half bathrooms, a gourmet kitchen you'll love, and it gotta fireplace in tha livin' room."

"Damn! When can I move down there wit y'all?"

"Whenever you're ready."

Unbeknownst to D-Mac, trouble had begun brewing for him as soon as he was spotted at the Exxon TigerMarket on Brick Church Pike.

"Is Kevin there?"

"This him. Who is this?"

"This Tae. You wouldn't believe who I just saw out East." He said.

"Who?"

"Remember dat nigga D-Mac, from Memphis?"

"Yeah." He replied. "He tha nigga dat knocked Lil' Paul for Ms. Morgan."

"Yup!" he confirmed. "I just saw him wit tha bitch."

"Yeah right! Where at?" Kevin inquired.

"At tha TigerMarket on Brick Church Pike at Trinity Lane."

"I bet you don't know where he went to."

"He in Madison now." Tae reported. "What you wanna do wit this nigga?"

"Where you at?"

"Jack-in-the-Box on Old Hickory Boulevard at Dickerson Road."

"I'm on my way."

RETRIBUTION&REVENGE**RETRIBUTION&REVENGE**RETRIBUTION&REVENGE

"Hey, D!" Candace called out from her bedroom. "You'll take me over my friend's house right quick?"

"What friend?"

"Brittany."

"When you wanna go?" he asked.

"We can go pick her up now, if you're ready."

"Momma know she comin' over here?" he asked cautiously.

"Yeah."

"Well, call her and let her know that we on tha way."

Candace placed the call, and told Brittany to be ready.

After a brief discussion, Rayne decided to remain at the house with her new mother-in-law. Plus, D-Mac's brothers were on their way over, and wanted to meet their new sister-in-law.

Candace's friend, Brittany, lived in South Nashville in the University Court housing projects.

As soon as they passed Jack-in-the-Box, preparing to jump onto I-65 South, D-Mac unknowingly picked up two tails: a 1998, white Cadillac Sedan Deville, and a 1998, grey Chevrolet Monte Carlo.

"You know what?" D-Mac asked Candace, as he prepare to exit the Interstate.

"It might just be me, but it seem like dat white 'Lac and dat grey Chevy been behind a nigga this whole time."

Candace flipped down the sun visor, using the vanity mirror to see what her brother was talking about.

Sure enough, as they exited the Interstate, so did the two vehicles they had been watching.

"I don't know who these niggaz is, or what they tryna pull, but they finna find start some shit they can't finish." D-Mac said, more to himself.

As he pulled into the drive, D-Mac noticed that only the Monte Carlo followed.

"Where Brittany stay at?" he asked.

"Near tha bottom of tha drive. Why?"

"Call and tell her we comin' in for a minute."

Candace placed the call, as they parked.

"Gone get out. I'll be out in a second." He told her.

When she climbed out of the car, D-Mac stuck his hand into the passenger seat, pulled it open, and removed a black backpack.

After closing the seat, he stepped from the car, and followed Candace to Brittany's apartment.

"What's wrong?" Brittany asked, as they walked into the door.

"I don't know." Candace responded. "These niggaz been followin' us since we was on tha Interstate."

Without a single word, D-Mac opened the backpack and emptied its contents onto the couch. There were two police-issue Kevlar vests, two shoulder holsters fitted for Desert Eagle pistols, and two .50 caliber Desert Eagle semi-automatic handguns, with four, thirty-round extended magazines.

"Here." He said, handing the vests to Candace and Brittany. "Put these on."

As they were putting on the vests, D-Mac removed his denim shirt, put on the shoulder holsters with the two .50 cal. Desert Eagles, and pulled the shirt back on without buttoning it up.

"Go sit in tha car." He told them, as he handed the keys to Candace. "I'm finna see what's up wit these niggaz. If it go down, when it's over, pull up to me and slide over quick."

As Candace and Brittany approached the car, D-Mac noticed the Monte Carlo parked a few spaces behind him, and the Cadillac was parked at the end of the drive. He decided to approach the Monte Carlo first.

"Hey my nigga!" he began. "What tha fuck you followin' me for?!"

"If I was followin' you, you'll know it." The man responded.

"You right." D-Mac answered, sarcastically. "I noticed you and tha 'Lac 'fore I got off tha Interstate."

The driver attempted to make a move, but decided against it when he felt the cold steel of the Desert Eagle pressed against his temple.

"You gotta death wish or something?" D-Mac asked. "Now, once again, why tha fuck y'all following' me?"

"South Central man!" he exclaimed. "Me, Tae and Lil' Paul had tha Morgan bitch movin' dat sack, but you knocked her, and she quit after you got out. Paul want yo head for dat."

D-Mac looked up just in time, to see the Cadillac bearing down upon him, the wrong way, up the drive. Quickly, he pulled the trigger, planting a round in Kevin's left temple. He them ran to the other side of the drive and began unloading both the Desert Eagles into the Cadillac and Tae.

As the Cadillac rolled to a stop, Candace pulled up in the Lexus.

"C'mon! Get in!" she yelled, as she jumped into the passenger seat.

Just as they got on the Interstate, D-Mac gave both pistols to Candace.

"Reload 'em, take those vests off, and put everything back in tha backpack." He instructed.

They followed his orders quickly and quietly.

"Get in tha back." He told Candace. "I gotta put this shit back up."

After he returned the backpack to its original location, and Candace had climbed back in the front seat, D-Mac placed an important phone call.

"Hello?" a female answered.

"Lemme talk to Letha!" He demanded.

"Who is this?" the female snapped back.

"Is this Jennifer?"

"Yeah! Who is this?" she asked again.

"This D-Mac!" he finally answered. "I need you and Letha to come to Nashville A.S.A.P.!"

"What you don' did now?"

"Murda, times two."

"Damn!" she exclaimed. "Can you go a year without gettin' in some shit?"

"I had a good reason." He responded. "Y'all just need to get here like yesterday!"

"Okay. Lay low. We on our way!"

Not only does his cousin Letha make wedding invitations, and other stationary, but she and her best friend, Jennifer, are successful criminal defense attorneys. They've been practicing law on their own for two years, and have remarkable trial records. Letha's record is 12-0, while Jennifer's is 18-1. Their record on cases they've worked together, is 6-0. They've become popular names in Memphis, and they've even won two cases together in Nashville, and it now appeared that they just received their third Nashville case.

Their secret to winning, is that they refuse to take a case unless there's at least an eighty percent chance of winning a trial, or a ninety percent chance of getting their clients the deals they want, or something better. They also have a mandatory requirement that their clients must disclose all facts, which are relevant to the cases, to be able to establish a reasonable defense.

RETRIBUTION&REVENGE**RETRIBUTION&REVENGE**RETRIBUTION&REVENGE

When D-Mac pulled into his father's driveway, he noticed that both of his brothers were there. When they walked into the house, he immediately informed everyone about what had transpired, and began to plan on how he could keep a low profile.

"Anyone of y'all gotta bank account?" D-Mac asked.

"I do." Twinn answered. "Why?"

"Because," he began, as he sat down at Candace's computer. "I'm finna make a wire transfer, and I'ma need you to go and withdraw the money, in cash."

"How much are you talkin' about?"

"$40,000 for now, but I want you to bring me $35,000 and you can keep tha extra $5,000."

"What am I supposed to say if they start askin' questions and shit?"

"Nothin'." D-Mac explained. "I'm gonna have a memo attached to the electronic request, stating that it's a business loan.'

"How you want it?"

"Large bills." He replied. "Fifties and hundred."

D-Mac pulled some money out of his pocket, and handed $100 to Redd.

"I need you to go to Auto Zone or somewhere, and get me a car cover." He instructed. "When they ask what kind of car, tell 'em a 2008 Toyota Avalon."

With everyone on their respective errands, there was nothing left to do, but wait.

RETRIBUTION&REVENGE**RETRIBUTION&REVENGE**RETRIBUTION&REVENGE

It was now two o'clock in the afternoon, and both Twinn and Redd had returned. While they were gone, D-Mac had called and asked Redd to pick up an AutoMart magazine on his way to the house.

After parking the Lexus in the backyard, and throwing the car cover over it, D-Mac began to browse the magazine, until he found something that caught his eye. The advertisement which stood out, read:

> **BUICK '95** Roadmaster Ltd. 5.4L V-8, turbo chrgd, P/W, P/DL, P/Seats, P/Steering, RKE, blk w/ grey lthr, 20" blk rims, 10% tint, cstm snd system. Invested $10K in all. 125K mi. Asking $12,500 o.b.o. Serious inq. only. Contact Shannon at 615-578-1746.

D-Mac immediately picked up the phone to place the call.

"Hello?" a female answered.

"May I speak with Shannon, please?" he asked.

"Hold on."

D-Mac removed the phone from his ear, as the woman screamed for Shannon to come to the phone. It took a minute, but she finally made it.

"Hello?"

"Shannon?"

"Speaking."

"This is D." he began. "I'm callin' about tha Roadmaster you got in tha AutoMart for sale."

"Oh, okay." She responded. "Actually, I have someone who's looking to buy it now."

"How much they willing to pay you for it?" he asked.

"Excuse me?"

"How much are they offerin', and do they have cash?"

"They've offered me $12,000 and yes, they have cash."

"What would you say if I told you that I got $12,000 in cash, and I'm willin' to raise it by $3,000?"

"You know what?" she stated, more than asked. "Let me see what they want to do."

D-Mac listened as she informed the potential buyers of his offer, as they attempted to renegotiate.

"Okay. They're willing to give me $18,000 for it."

"Will you tell 'em to take a walk, if I offered you $20,000?" he asked. "Because that's as high as I'm willin' to go."

When she relayed the message, D-Mac was relieved at what he heard next.

"Right now, I'm in Hendersonville." She explained. "Where would you like to meet?"

"How 'bout Pep Boys in Rivergate?" he suggested. Is dat straight with you?"

"That's fine." She agreed. "What time?"

"How 'bout now?"

"Okay. I'll see you in about fifteen minutes."

With an appointed time set, he hopped in the car with Twinn, and they headed to Rivergate.

RETRIBUTION&REVENGERETRIBUTION&REVENGE**RETRIBUTION&REVENGE**

When they pulled in, Shannon was already there, the Roadmaster looking like a thing of beauty. She stepped from the car and introduced herself, and her sister, who had followed her there.

"I'm Shannon, and this is my sister, Telisha."

"I'm D-Mac, and this is my brother, Twinn." He responded. "So, this is it, huh?"

He asked the question kind of matter-of-factly, without taking his eyes off Shannon's. Even though he was married, he couldn't help but to admire the beauty before him. There she stood at 5'5", weighing approximately 145 to 150 pounds. She had a radiantly beautiful caramel complexion, shoulder length black hair with light brown highlights, and the most beautiful and seductive honey brown eyes he had ever seen. In all actuality, she would've been the perfect model to represent the adjective of gorgeous.

"Yeah! This is it." She responded, flashing her brilliant, pearly whites. "C'mon, let's take it for a spin."

As they got into the Roadmaster, with D-Mac behind the wheel, Shannon told Telisha to hang out with Twinn for a while.

"He won't bite." D-Mac teased. "Unless you want him to!"

They headed past Rivergate Mall and jumped on the Interstate. As they were returning, Shannon decided that she would rather take detour.

"Look," she began. "You see it rides and handles good to be fourteen years old, but let's head to the mall."

"What you got on your mind?" D-Mac asked.

"It's my turn to take a test drive." She responded, as she ran her hand up his inner thigh.

D-Mac had refused plenty of other advances from women after he and Rayne had exchanged their vows, but there was something extraordinarily different about this gorgeous woman. As though he was under a hypnotic spell, he granted her wish, and pulled into the Mall's parking lot.

"Find somewhere to park, then follow me." She said, as she climbed into the back seat. "Look under the passenger seat, and you'll see a sun visor to put in the front windshield."

When he parked, and placed the visor in the windshield as instructed, he turned around to discover, to his amazement, that Shannon was completely naked and waiting.

"You don't waste no time, do you?" he asked, as he climbed into the back seat with her.

"Why should I?" she replied. "I have what you want, and you have what I *need*!"

"I got what you need?" he asked, kind of puzzled.

"Baby, I have an extremely healthy sexual appetite." She explained. "When I saw the way you looked at me back there, it turned me on so much, that I had to have you.'

"If you need it, you finna get it."

"First, take off all your clothes." She demanded. "I saw the ring, and I don't want you getting in trouble with your wife. Here's a condom, and I have some handy-wipes in my purse for afterwards."

With that, being said, D-Mac stripped down, strapped up, and dove in. He wasn't trying to make love to her, because he guessed that he'd never see her again.

He put her legs on his shoulders and commenced to thrashing her, as though there was not tomorrow.

"Oh, baby!" she yelled. "That's what I'm talkin' about! Fuck me harder baby!" Fuck he HARDER!"

D-Mac switched into overdrive.

"This ain't what you want."

"Yes, it is! Yes, it is!" she replied, with a slight growl. "Talk to me baby, please!"

"Shut tha fuck up." He complied. "While I beat this pussy up!"

He raised up, planting her feet firmly against the door on either side of her head.

"Who pussy is this?" he demanded. "And don't make me have to ask you again!"

"It's yours baby!"

"What's my name?"

"D!" she yelled.

"Naw!" he replied, as he smacked her on her ass. "Call me Daddy!"

"Okay Daddy!"

"What's – My – Name?" he demanded, accentuating each word with rough, deep thrusts.

"It's Daddy!" she exclaimed. "Oh, my God! It's Daddy!"

"Is this how you want it?" he asked.

"Yes Daddy!"

"This ain't how you want it." He told her, as he pulled out. "Turn yo ass around and get on all fours!"

She complied with the orders given, and he began to fuck her from the back.

"Now, is this how you want it?"

"No Daddy!"

"Tell me how you want it then."

"Pull my hair Daddy!" she demanded.

D-Mac wrapped both of his hands within her hair, yanking her head back with each thrust. Her pussy was so wet, that D-Mac could feel her inner juices saturating his groin area and running down his legs.

"Take this dick!" he shouted. "This what you wanted, ain't it?"

"Yes Daddy! Yes! Yes! Oh, yes!" she yelled, as she reached her climax. "Keep goin'! Don't stop! Yes! Right there Daddy! Ahhhhhh!"

They both collapsed onto the back seat, after reaching their destination.

"Damn girl!" D-Mac exclaimed. "You a beast! We gotta do this again sometime."

"Well," she began, as she pulled several handy-wipes from her purse. "We can, if you come back to Nashville, or if you're not in prison."

"What you talkin' about, if I'm not in prison?" he asked, defensively.

"They had your picture on the news." She explained. "They say you're a suspect in that double murder in U.C. earlier."

"Really?"

"Yeah. I knew who you were the moment you stepped out of the car."

"I guess you gon' turn me in, huh?" he asked.

"Why?" she asked him. "You just bought my car for $7,500 more than what I was originally asking for it, *AND*, you gave me some great sex! Not to mention you want to hook again! So, why would I turn you in?"

"You make a good argument." He agreed.

"Plus," Shannon continued. "I figured you might need a good defense attorney."

"You talkin' about hiring me an attorney?"

"No." she laughed. "I'm talkin' about *being* your attorney."

"Are you serious?" D-Mac asked.

"Sure!" she confirmed. "Been practicing for about eight years now."

"If you don't mind me askin', how old are you?"

"I'll be thirty-four in August."

"What's your track record at trial?"

"Right now," she paused, as she scrolled her memory. "It's 32-4-5."

"What's that supposed to mean?"

"It means that I've won thirty-two cases at trial, lost four, and had five end with either a mistrial or a hung jury. And," she continued. "The reason I lost those four, was because my clients weren't completely honest with me about facts of their cases."

"So, what would you charge me for a double homicide?" he asked. "If I brought in three individuals to assist you?"

"It depends. Who are the three individuals?'

"Two prominent attorneys from Memphis and a Certified Legal Assistant."

"Names?"

"Tha attorneys are Letha Latham and Jennifer Echols."

"You're kidding?!" she asked, in disbelief.

"No." he replied. "Letha's my cousin and Jennifer's her best friend and legal partner. As a matter-of-fact, they should be pulling into Nashville in tha next hour or so."

"And the Paralegal?"

"Me!" he replied, as he climbed back into the driver's seat, and removed the sun visor. "I'm certified through Blackstone Career Institute, plus, I have six years' experience as a Jailhouse Lawyer in TDOC."

"I tell you what." She began, as they pulled out into traffic. "Whenever you come to Nashville, and whenever I go to Memphis, if you can promise me the same great sex you just gave me, that plus $10,000 should be enough."

"That's what's up." He agreed.

RETRIBUTION&REVENGE**RETRIBUTION&REVENGE**RETRIBUTION&REVENGE

Twinn and Telisha were sitting in Telisha's BMW 325i when they returned.

"I bet they wonderin' where tha hell we been at!" D-Mac laughed.

"Your brother probably was, but Telisha already knew what was up."

D-Mac gave her the $20,000 for the car, plus $10,000 as a retainer.

"Just give me $5,000 now, then, you can give me the other $5,000 when I sign on as your attorney." She told him, as she handed $5,000 back to him.

"That's what's up." He replied. "I'll call you as soon as I hear something from Letha and Jennifer."

"Alright. Talk to you later."

Before they pulled off, Twinn wanted answers, and in detail.

"What tha hell was that?" he asked.

"What?"

"You know what I'm talkin' about!" he shot back, with a smirk on his face. "What's with tha five stacks now, and five stacks later? You payin' for pussy now?"

"Hell naw!" D-Mac responded quickly. "She's an attorney, and she gon' be on my defense team."

"So, what's her last name?"

"Swift. Shannon Swift."

"When we get to the house, I'ma call information, and see what they say.

"Call it now." D-Mac offered. "It's 615-555-1212."

When Twinn called, and asked for the listing, he put it on speakerphone, so D-Mac could hear it.

"The number is: 615-860-1324. Again…."

Before Twinn could say anything, D-Mac had already dialed the number. When he reached the voicemail, he put it on speakerphone.

"You have reached the Law Office of Shannon Swift. I'm either on the phone, away from my desk, or the office. You may try me on my cell phone at 615-578-1746. Otherwise, leave a message, and I'll return your call at my earliest convenience."

"So," D-Mac began. "the cell number she gave is tha same one she used in tha AutoMart ad. What a coincidence!"

They both hopped into their cars and headed to tha house.

Just as they pulled into the driveway, D-Mac's phone rang.

"Hello?"

"We in Nashville." It was Jennifer. "Where we need to get off at?"

"Follow tha Clarksville signs, and get off at Trinity Lane."

"Then what?"

Swing a left and meet me at tha TigerMarket." He explained. "I'ma be in a black, '95 Roadmaster on some black twenties."

"Okay. See you we get there."

D-Mac went in the house and grabbed Rayne.

"C'mon." He told her. "Letha and Jennifer just pulled in tha 'Ville. We gotta go meet 'em."

They jumped into the newly acquired Roadmaster, and took the back roads to the TigerMarket. On the way there, he called Shannon.

RETRIBUTION&REVENGE**RETRIBUTION&REVENGE**RETRIBUTION&REVENGE

"You couldn't wait, could you?" she asked, teasingly.

"Hey!" he jumped in. "My wife and I finna meet Letha and Jennifer at tha TigerMarket on Trinity Lane, at Brick Church Pike. How quick can you get there?"

"How's twenty minutes?"

"See you then."

"Who was that?" Rayne asked.

"That's tha woman I bought this car from." He explained. "She's a local, criminal-defense attorney, wit eight years under her belt."

"How did you find that out?"

"Well, when I was test-drivin', she kinda confessed to me."

"About what?"

"That they already had my face plastered on tha news 'bout tha double homi." He explained. "She saw it, so when we met up 'bout tha car, she instantly knew who I was."

"So, she offered to help you out?"

"Yeah. For ten racks, plus some assistance."

"What kind of assistance?"

"Two additional attorneys and a Certified Paralegal."

"So, you, Letha and Jennifer?"

"Yup!" he responded with a smile. "The ultimate dream team!"

RETRIBUTION&REVENGE**RETRIBUTION&REVENGE**RETRIBUTION&REVENGE

When they arrived at the TigerMarket, they sat there for ten minutes before Shannon showed up. She approached the car, climbed into the back seat, and introduced herself to Rayne.

"Hi." She spoke, as she offered her hand to Rayne. "I'm Shannon Swift, and I'll be assisting your husband with his forthcoming case.

"I'm Rayne" she responded, "Nice to meet you."

"While we're waiting for them to get here, what's the maximum bond you can post right now?"

"I can make a $300,000 bond, if it ain't a cash bond."

"Okay." She responded, as she took noted on her legal pad. "Now, if requested by the D.A., would you be willing to relocate to Nashville until after the trial?"

"If tha D.A. makes that a stipulation so I can stay outta jail, then sure."

As she was taking note of that, Letha and Jennifer pulled into the parking lot.

"There they go." He informed Shannon. "Where would be a good place for all of us to discuss this without being notice?"

"Get them to get two separate rooms at tha Knight's Inn." She explained. "Preferably next door to each other."

He relayed the information when they walked to the car. Afterwards, Shannon hopped in her car, and they followed one another down the street to the Knight's Inn.

RETRIBUTION&REVENGE**RETRIBUTION&REVENGE**RETRIBUTION&REVENGE

"So," Letha began, after formal introductions were made. "Tell us what happened."

"I was takin' Candace to pick up her friend, Brittany, from U.C. out South." He began explaining. "Before I got to my exit, I peeped a Monte Carlo and a 'Lac following me. So, when we got to U.C., and I pulled in tha drive, tha Monte Carlo followed, but tha 'Lac went to tha bottom of tha drive, like he was gon' box me in or somethin'.

"We went in Brittany's house, I strapped up and went to tha nigga in tha Monte Carlo. I asked him why he was followin' me, and he acted like he wanted to buck, so I put tha pistol to his dome."

"Did he tell you why they were following you?" Shannon asked.

"Yeah." He responded coldly, looking at Rayne. "I was locked up wit both of 'em at South Central."

"Who was it?" Rayne asked.

"It was Kevin and Tae." He answered. "Evidently, Lil' Paul put a tag on my head, because I knocked you from him."

"Are you serious?" she exclaimed.

"Yeah. Apparently, they had you movin' they sack, and I came along and took you from Lil' Paul, and now he want my head for it." He continued, glaring at Rayne, with a mixture of anger and disbelief.

"What happened after he told you that?" Jennifer asked, sensing the mixed emotions in D-Mac's eyes.

"I turned to see tha 'Lac comin' tha wrong way up tha drive towards me, so I popped one off at Kevin in tha Monte Carlo, then I unloaded both tha Eagles in tha 'Lac 'fore it finally stopped. Then, I jumped in tha car and dipped."

"What time is it?" Letha asked.

"Five till five." Shannon answered. "Why?"

"Tha news." D-Mac spoke up. "Channel 5."

They turned the television to News Channel 5, and waited for the five o'clock news broadcast to begin.

"Good evening. I'm Vicki Yates. We have some breaking news to tell you about. At around noon today, Metro police responded to a call of shots fired in the University Court housing development. When they arrived,

they found two deceased victims, in their vehicles. Here's Nicole Ferguson with more."

"Thanks Vicki. Metro says twenty-six-year-old Kevin Gilmore, was found with a single gunshot wound to the head, in his 1987 Chevrolet Monte Carlo. The second victim, thirty-two-year-old DeVontè Madison, was found with multiple gunshot wounds to his body and head, in his 1998 Cadillac Sedan Deville. They both had been released from prison within the last four months.

"Now, witnesses told police that the shooter fled in a champagne-colored, newer model Lexus with large, chrome wheels, and personalized, Shelby County plates, which reads 'F-U-K-A-H-8-R.' The registration, per Metro, comes back to a Derrick Franklin, also a parolee, who was released nearly a year ago, and resides in Memphis. Police still aren't clear as to what Franklin was doing in Nashville. Reporting live from South Nashville, I'm Nicole Ferguson, News Channel 5 HD."

"The spokesperson for Metro says that because of the high caliber weapon used, Derrick Franklin is to be considered armed and extremely dangerous. They stress that the recklessness with which Franklin fired his weapon, is one clear indication as to how callous and reckless an individual he is. A total of sixty, .50 caliber shell casings were retrieved from the scene.

"Police speculate that because Gilmore received one gunshot wound to the head, the other fifty-nine were fired into Madison and his Cadillac. The police urge the public to help get this individual off the streets.

"Also, tonight ..."

After turning off turning off the television, they all sat in silence, lost in their own thoughts.

"So, what now?" D-Mac asked. "They makin' me look like some fuckin' monster! They don't even know what tha fuck really happened!"

"What do you wanna do?" Letha asked.

"I wanna clean up tha Lex, drive it downtown, and turn myself in." He explained. "Maybe I can argue mistaken identity. Of course, I'ma have y'all follow me down there."

"Let's give it a try." Letha agreed.

RETRIBUTION&REVENGE**RETRIBUTION&REVENGE**RETRIBUTION&REVENGE

When he returned to his father's house, D-Mac removed the guns and vests from the car, gave them to Twinn for safekeeping, jumped in the Lexus, and returned to the hotel.

"What if they wanna know why they're up here from Memphis?" Rayne asked, with concern.

"I'll tell 'em that when I caught wind of tha bullshit, I told 'em to get up here so I can turn myself in, and get this shit cleared up."

"What about Candace and Brittany?"

"I already got that covered." He explained. "I took Candace to pick up Brittany, and we left. I didn't have no pistol, and I ain't shoot not pistol."

After taking a shower and washing his hands with bleach, then ammonia (which he had Shannon to purchase), they caravanned to the Criminal Justice Center, with Shannon in the lead, and Letha and Jennifer bringing up the rear.

When they hit Second Avenue North, and parked in front of the Justice Center, officers and civilians alike gawked at the sight. The man whom the police and media declared extremely dangerous, had just parked his luxurious "getaway" car in front of the Justice

Center, and appeared to be turning himself in, accompanied with three prominent attorneys.

In addition to that, D-Mac had insisted that the media be alerted ahead of time, so that his surrender would be captured on video. He figured it would play well for a jury, if he was to end up going to trial again.

"Hey!" an officer called out, not sure if his eyes were deceiving him. "Ain't you Derrick Franklin?"

"Yeah." He replied. "This is my wife, and these are my attorneys. I'm comin' to turn myself in, so I can get this bullshit cleared up and straightened out."

They entered the building and proceeded to the Robbery/Homicide Division's Office, with about a half-dozen officers following them.

"Can I help you?" a passing detective asked.

"I need to speak wit tha detective ova tha double homicides in U.C." D-Mac responded.

"And you are?"

"I'm Derrick Franklin." He answered. "Your alleged suspect."

"Um, follow me." She instructed him, in disbelief.

She led them to a room, and told them to have a seat. She then, escorted Rayne to a nearby waiting area.

"They'll be with you in a minute." She informed them.

RETRIBUTION&REVENGE**RETRIBUTION&REVENGE**RETRIBUTION&REVENGE

"So, Mr. Franklin." The detective began. "I'm Detective Davenport, and as you know, I'm investigating that double homicide you've been implicated in. What can you tell me about it?"

"Nothin'."

"So, why are people naming you as the shooter?"

"I don't know. Why don't you ask 'em?"

"Actually, I'm asking you."

"Look man," D-Mac exclaimed, showing obvious frustration and irritation. "If I had done that bullshit, do you actually think I woulda came down here and turned myself in?"

"I don't know. Would you?"

"I came down here, 'cause y'all got me all on tha fuckin' news, like I'm some kinda murderous psychopath!" D-Mac exclaimed. "I just wanna get my name cleared, so I can finish my vacation. I just pulled in tha 'Ville, and already, it's some bullshit!"

"Speaking of vacation," the detective prodded on. "Why did you come to Nashville in the first place?"

"Today is my wife's birthday, and I figga'd I'll brang her up here to meet my dad's side of tha family." He replied.

"What were you doin' in University Court?"

"I went to pick up a friend, then I left." He answered. "I didn't shoot nobody, and I didn't kill nobody. *PERIOD!*"

"Then tell me why I have at least four witnesses who say that you walked up and shot that guy in the head for nothing, then unloaded on the Cadillac?"

"I don't know why they told you that. Maybe they saw my Shelby County tags and didn't like what they say."

"What do they say?"

"You already know what they say!" D-Mac retorted. "Hell, you put tha shit all on tha fuckin' news!"

"F-U-K-A-H-8-R," the detective read. "Look like a bunch of mumbo jumbo to me."

"Well, it's not!" he shot back. "It's an acronym for 'Fuck A Hata'!"

"Oh! Okay, look." The detective continued, obviously with a trick up his sleeve. "We already know what happened. Who knows? You may have had a legitimate reason to do what you did, but we can't know that until you talk to us."

"Lemme tell you somethin'!" D-Mac shouted. "If you had anything otha than some bullshit statements, we wouldn't be havin' this bullshit conversation!"

"Now, calm down Mr. Franklin."

"Fuck dat!" he shot back. "You got one of two choices! Either charge me, or let me go! Anythang else you wanna say, say it to my lawyers!"

"I'll be right back." The detective said, as he stood up and left the interrogation room.

He returned a few minutes later, with three detectives in tow.

"Stand up and put your hands behind your back." Detective Davenport demanded.

"What are you charging him with?" Jennifer asked.

"He's being charged with two counts of First-Degree Murder; Unlawful Possession of a Firearm by a Convicted Felon; Unlawful Possession of a Firearm with Felony Intent; and forty counts of Reckless Endangerment." The other detective responded.

"Mr. Franklin," Detective Davenport began. "You have the right to remain silent. Anything you say, can and will be used against you in a court of law. You have the right to have an attorney present during questioning. If you cannot afford an attorney, one will be appointed to you. Do you understand your rights?"

"Of course," D-Mac answered. "When will I be arraigned and receive a bond?"

"In a couple of hours."

"I'll make some calls." Shannon told D-Mac. "I'll see if I can cash in some favors, and get you an immediate video arraignment."

"I'll call up a few bonding companies." Letha added.

"And I'll prepare the pre-trial motions and a Motion for Discovery." Jennifer chimed in.

RETRIBUTION&REVENGE**RETRIBUTION&REVENGE**RETRIBUTION&REVENGE

"Franklin! You got arraignment!" the officer called out.

D-Mac followed the officer into night court, where Letha, Jennifer and Shannon were waiting for him.

"Mr. Franklin." The Judge began. "I see you're more than capable of affording an attorney. To the charges of two counts of First-Degree Murder; Unlawful Possession of a Firearm by a Convicted Felon; Unlawful Possession of a Firearm with Felony Intent; and forty counts of Reckless Endangerment, how do you plead?"

"Not guilty on all counts Your Honor." D-Mac replied.

"We would like to request bail for the Defendant, Your Honor." Jennifer stated.

"The State would like to request remand, due to the seriousness of the charges alleged against the Defendant." The Assistant District Attorney argued.

"Mr. Franklin is a respected businessman in his hometown of Memphis." Letha countered. "He also has tremendous family support both in Memphis and in Nashville."

"Bail is set at $2 Million cash." The Judge ordered.

"Your Honor," D-Mac interjected. "Tha evidence they have is circumstantial at best. They have no murder weapon, no physical evidence connecting me to the alleged crime, whatsoever. Outside of witness statements they claim to have from alleged witnesses, they cannot place any type of weapon in my hand; much less prove that I am the shooter."

"Are you going to allow your legal team to make any arguments for you Mr. Franklin?" the Judge interrupted.

"I *am* part of my legal team." He responded. "I'ma Certified Paralegal, licensed to practice in the states of Tennessee, Alabama, and Kentucky."

"Alright. Continue."

"Aside from the fact that I voluntarily turned myself in, upon seeing my face plastered on the news, the Eighth Amendment of the United States Constitution specifically reads that 'excessive bail *shall not* be required, nor excessive fines imposed, nor cruel and unusual punishment inflicted.' And, considering the lack of concrete evidence, $2 Million is extremely excessive."

"Do the State have a response?" the Judge asked.

"No, Your Honor."

"Well, bail is now set at $150,000 cash or bond." He ordered.

"Is that better Mr. Franklin?"

"Yes, Your Honor." He replied. "Thank you."

RETRIBUTION&REVENGERETRIBUTION&REVENGE**RETRIBUTION&REVENGE**

"I got a bonding company for you." Letha informed him, during their attorney visit.

"See if they'll take $7,500 cash now." He told her. "If not, tell 'em to come get me, and I'll give 'em ten racks now, then tha otha five when I can get to tha bank Monday mornin'."

"Will do."

She left the visiting area to join the bondsman, who was waiting outside, to get D-Mac out on bond. D-Mac, on the other hand, was headed back to his cell, until they could get the paperwork together for his release. Lucky for him, his cousin was his parole officer, so he didn't have to worry about getting violated.

RETRIBUTION&REVENGE**RETRIBUTION&REVENGE**RETRIBUTION&REVENGE

"Franklin!" an officer called out. "Pack it up! You're outta here!"

D-Mac jumped up and grabbed his property, which was nothing more than the kit they gave him in booking. He hadn't unpacked, because he knew that he would be making bond.

"Hey baby!" Rayne greeted him. "How are you feeling?"

"Glad to be up outta there." He replied. "What y'all come up with?"

"Well," Shannon began. "I've set up a meeting with the A.D.A. for Monday morning. Hopefully, we can come up with a reasonable solution."

"What's tha deal on tha bond situation?" he asked. "How much is tha damage?"

"They took the $7,500." Letha spoke up.

"Yeah! Only after Shannon signed her name as the responsible party." Jennifer chimed in.

"So, what's next?"

"The only thing I'd suggest is that you keep a low profile for a few days, until after we meet with the A.D.A." Shannon advised.

"So, how long before I can expect to return to Memphis?"

"We'll know once we meet with the A.D.A."

"Alright. It's late, and I'm tired as fuck!" D-Mac exclaimed. "We gon' get a room at tha Opryland Hotel. I'll holla back at y'all tomorrow."

"Stay outta trouble this weekend!" Jennifer teased.

"Hell, he get in anything else, they won't give him another bond!" Letha added.

"Not unless he bribes a judge!" Shannon laughed.

They all got into their cars and left, but not before finalizing some paperwork with the bonding company.

"Are you hungry?" Rayne asked, as they settled into their suite.

"No. I just wanna take a shower and got to sleep."

They both took their showers and turned in for the night.

Sunday, April 12, 2009

Rayne woke up just as D-Mac was returning from an errand, around eight o'clock.

"Where you been baby?" she asked.

"I had to make a coupla runs." He told her. "I ain't been in tha 'Ville twenty-four hours, and I done already had to burn over thirty-two racks!"

"I don't like tha tone in your voice." Rayne expressed. "What are you planning on doing?"

"I got $2,000 cash, and I need to take care of some business."

"What kind of business?"

"It's nothin' you need to worry 'bout." He answered. "Just be cool. I'll be back later."

RETRIBUTION&REVENGE**RETRIBUTION&REVENGE**RETRIBUTION&REVENGE

D-Mac picked up a pre-paid cell phone at a nearby Walgreens, and activated it under a false name. He placed a couple of phone calls while he was on his way to his sister's house in Englewood.

"Yo, Twinn."

"What's up lil' bruh?"

"Where you at now?" D-Mac asked his brother. "I need to swang through and get those Eagles."

"Where you want me to meet you?"

"You can meet me at Ellen's." He responded. "I'm headin' over there now."

"A'ight. See you in a few."

After disconnecting the call, he called Candace.

"Hello?" a female voice answered.

"Where Candace?"

"Hold on." She told him, as she called for her.

"What's up?"

"Hey, I need you to do me a huge favor." He informed her. I'ma take care of you."

"What is it?" she asked.

"I need you to drive tha Roadmaster over to Ellen's."

"When?"

"I'm on my way over there right now."

"A'ight." She replied. "I'll meet you there."

RETRIBUTION&REVENGE**RETRIBUTION&REVENGE**RETRIBUTION&REVENGE

D-Mac and Twinn both arrived at Ellen's within minutes of each other.

"You want 'em now?" Twinn asked.

"No, not yet." D-Mac responded. "Candace on her way over here in tha Roadmaster."

"What you finna do?"

"I just got some business to take care of. Nothin' major."

As they were talking, Candace pulled up in the Roadmaster, with Brittany riding with her.

"What's up lil' sis?"

"Nothin' much." She replied. "Here's your car, now what you got for me?"

"Here you go." He said, as he handed her six crisp, one hundred-dollar bills. "Plus, I'ma let you drive tha Lexus for a while."

"That's what's up!" she exclaimed. "How long you gon' let me keep it?"

"I don't know yet." He answered. "Just be careful, and *DO NOT* drive to U.C. or J.C.!"

"Why not?" she asked.

"What happened out there yesterday?" he reminded her.

"But I thought they let you go 'cause they dropped tha charges?"

"No. They let me go 'cause I posted a $150,000 bond." He explained. "Plus, if they see tha car, they'll probably follow you, so be careful about where you go and what you do. Not to mention those niggaz probably got friends who'll love to get revenge."

"A'ight."

After spending an hour or so with Ellen and her family, D-Mac set out to take care of some quite volatile business.

"Hello?" a female answered.

"Is Osha there?" D-Mac asked.

"Yeah. Hold on." She responded, before clicking over to clear the other line.

"What's up?" a male voice answered.

"Osha?"

"Yeah."

"This D-Mac. You busy?"

"Naw. Where you at?"

"I'm in tha 'Ville." He responded. "Where would be a good spot to meet?"

"What side of town you on?"

"Englewood."

"A'ight. Meet me at tha Family Fun Center in Hendersonville."

"I'll be there in twenty, locked and loaded."

"That's what's up."

As he headed to Hendersonville, D-Mac placed another call to arrange another meeting.

"What's tha business?" a man answered.

"Chase?"

"Who is this?"

"D-Mac."

"What's up fool?"

"Nothin' much." D-Mac replied. "What's tha chance of you meetin' me and Osha in Hendersonville?"

"When?"

"I'm headin' there now." He replied. "Tha Family Fun Center, suited and ready."

"I can be there in like, thirty minutes."

"A'ight. See you there."

D-Mac knew that once he met up with these two individuals, everything else would come together.

D-Mac met Osha and Chase when he served his time at South Central. They had endless conversations about robberies and home invasions, that would be extremely easy, with an enormous payout. They had a pre-constructed plan to alleviate all problems which may arise: call; meet; discuss; execute; divide; and disperse.

While D-Mac and Osha waited on Chase, they decided to play a few games of pool.

RETRIBUTION&REVENGE**RETRIBUTION&REVENGE**RETRIBUTION&REVENGE

"So, what you been up to?" Osha asked.

"Not shit!" he responded. "I come to tha 'Ville and ain't been here twenty-four hours, and I done already caught two bodies! How's that for a vacation?"

"Damn! I thought that was you I saw on tha news." Osha replied. "Plus, this gal I fuck wit who stay in U.C. was tellin' me about it."

"What she say happened?"

"She said some nigga in a Lexus sittin' big was actin' a fool wit two Desert Eagles." He recalled. "She said dat shit was like somethin' you see in tha movies, only those was real bullets, and they was fuckin' shit up!"

"What else she say about it?"

"She said he had personalized tags from Shelby County."

"What tha business is?" someone called out from across the area.

It was the final individual they had been waiting on. Chase.

"You know. Time to get dat paper!" D-Mac responded.

"What y'all got in mind?"

"Well." D-Mac began. "You probably done already heard 'bout those two bodies in U.C."

"Yeah. How much was yo bond on dat?" Chase asked.

"$150,000, but I found a bonding company to fuck wit me for $7,500, plus, one of my lawyers had to sign tha bond."

"Who you got?" Osha asked.

"I got Letha Latham and Jennifer Echols from Memphis, and Shannon Swift from tha 'Ville."

"You got Shannon Swift *and* those two big-shots from Memphis?" Osha asked, in disbelief.

"Yeah. I had to get tha best." D-Mac replied. "Letha's my cousin, Jennifer's her best friend, plus, I signed myself on to help Shannon as her Paralegal."

"Damn!" Chase exclaimed. "So, you get to see and handle *all* tha original evidence the State got, if you go to trial."

"Hell yeah!" D-Mac responded. "Plus, I'll be able to see tha list of witnesses tha State plan to call, prior to tha trial."

"Who knows what could happen if dat list falls in tha wrong hands." Osha laughed.

"Precisely. Now," D-Mac continued. "I been in Nashville twenty-four hours, and I done spent damn-near forty stacks already. So, since I'm stuck here, and can't go back to tha 'M', I need to bounce back."

"You know, I got this gal who been fuckin' wit some big-time dope boy out North." Osha offered.

"How big?" Chase asked.

"I'll tell you in a minute." He replied, as he picked up his phone, and began dialing.

"What's up?" What you doin'? … Nothin' much. Hey, what kinda weight dude playin' wit? … Fa real? … You at tha house now? … Anybody else there wit y'all? … What he got in tha crib now? … You sho'? … A'ight. Dat's what's up."

"So, what's tha word?" D-Mac asked.

"She said dat they at tha house now, by theyself, and tha nigga just went to re-up, and he got a hundred and fifty pounds of Loud, ten keys of white, and a shit-load of pills."

"Damn!" D-Mac and Chase both exclaimed.

"What about cash?" D-Mac asked.

"She said he got a safe and he keep at least a quarta mill in it."

"We gon' need a truck to get all dat shit up outta there." Chase advised.

"Don't worry." D-Mac assured him. "I got dat covered."

"How we gon' do this?" Osha asked.

"We can go in like tha Feds or tha Vice. I still got my .50 cals, but I only got two vests." D-Mac explained.

"I gotta vest." Chase offered. "I gotta coupla K's too."

"A'ight. We can use 'em." D-Mac responded. "Everybody need to be in all black. Black pants, black t-shirts, black hats, and black shoes. What kinda pistols y'all got?"

"I gotta Glock .40 and a Glock 9." Chase answered.

"I gotta coupla 7's and a .44." Osha added.

"Brang both of those Glocks." D-Mac instructed. "I'll see if I can find a SUV or somethin'. What y'all drivin'?"

"I'm in my Impala." Chase answered.

"I'm in a two-door Cutlass." Osha added.

"A'ight. We gon' meet up at tha Hallmark Inn on Trinity Lane." D-Mac told them. "We'll finish tha preparations there. I'll text y'all wit tha room number."

"What time we gon' meet?" Chase asked.

"Five o'clock."

"Dat's what's up." Osha agreed.

At that point, they went their separate ways, to prepare for the upcoming heist.

RETRIBUTION&REVENGE**RETRIBUTION&REVENGE**RETRIBUTION&REVENGE

D-Mac arrived at the Hallmark Inn at a quarter to five. He had located a 1987 Chevrolet Suburban at a gas station in Madison. He filled the tank in Englewood, and was now waiting on the rest of the crew to arrive.

Osha was the first to arrive, followed several minutes later by Chase.

"So, where tha house at?" D-Mac asked.

"It's an apartment on Herman Street." Osha responded. "Old girl said dat on Sundays, dude don't do shit, so they'll be there by theyself."

"When we gon' hit 'em?" Chase asked.

"Will 7 o'clock be straight?" D-Mac asked Osha.

"Lemme check."

After a brief conversation with his contact, Osha confirmed that it was a go.

"A'ight. Let's do this." D-Mac encouraged.

D-Mac climbed into the Suburban, while Chase and Osha followed in the Impala.

When they arrived near the apartment complex, they parked a couple of buildings down, and proceeded ahead on foot.

"Chase, you hit tha door," D-Mac instructed. "Osha, you come in behind me."

When they approached the door, D-Mac began banging with his fist.

"Police!" he yelled. "Open up! We have a search warrant!"

Upon hearing someone moving around inside, Chase kicked the door open, and D-Mac, with Osha behind him, ran in with his weapons drawn.

"Get yo ass on tha muthafuckin' floor, and put yo hands behind yo head!" D-Mac ordered the man and the woman, whom he encountered upon entry.

"What tha fuck is all this shit about?" the man inquired.

"Just sit there and shut tha fuck up!" Chase yelled.

"Where tha money and tha dope at?" D-Mac demanded.

"I don't know what you talkin' 'bout!" the man pleaded.

"Where it's at?" he asked the woman.

"I don't know nothin' 'bout no dope!" she cried.

Osha grabbed her by her hair, and began to drag her, kicking and screaming, to the back bedroom.

"Look man," D-Mac tried to reason. "I don't wanna hurt nobody, but I ain't fucked up wit it. Now, just tell me where tha shit at, and I'll let you live to see anotha day."

"Fuck you!" the man replied.

D-Mac looked at Osha, laughed, then shot the man in the leg.

"Now, dat was just a warnin' shot." D-Mac told him. "How many more of these .50s can you take? Huh?"

"Okay! Okay!" he replied, crying. "Tha dope is in tha corner of tha attic, and tha money is in my safes!"

After retrieving the drugs from the attic, they took the man into the bedroom, where he had two floor safes, and a gun safe.

"Combinations!" D-Mac demanded. "For all three!"

When they opened the floor safes, both were filled with stacks of fifty and hundred-dollar bills. In the gun safe, he had a small lockbox filled with assorted, diamond-encrusted jewelry, including watches, rings, bracelets, necklaces, and pendants. In the gun safe, there were two SKS assault rifles, an AR-15 assault rifle, two Mack-11s, an M-16 assault rifle, and an AK-47 assault rifle. In a

Dolce & Gabana handbag, they found three Glock 19 9mms, two Beretta 85 ACP .380s, and three Glock 22 .40s. They proceeded to place what they found beside the front door.

"I'm finna go get tha truck." D-Mac told them. "I'll be right back."

After backing the Suburban up to the building, and loading it up with the drugs, money, weapons, and electronics, they left the man tied up in the bedroom, and took the woman in the living room.

"Wait about thirty minutes, then act like you got yo'self loose, 'fore you untie him." Osha told her. "I'll get up wit you later."

They met back up at the Hallmark Inn. After transferring everything into the hotel room, D-Mac had Chase to follow him in his Roadmaster, as they went to dump the Suburban.

First, they purchased five gallons of gasoline, then, they took the SUV to an area known as Westchester, where they completely doused the interior. Finally, to complete the mission, D-Mac struck a match, and lit the covers of three matchbooks, tossing one on the front seat, one on the back seat, and one in the cargo area. He left all the windows down, so that the flames could be fed by plenty of oxygen from the outside.

"Let's dip." D-Mac said, as he climbed in the car.

As they turned onto Brick Church Pike, they could see the flames dancing inside of the Suburban.

RETRIBUTION&REVENGE**RETRIBUTION&REVENGE**RETRIBUTION&REVENGE

When they arrived back at the Hallmark Inn, they began to inventory their take. The final count was $340,000 in cash, two hundred pounds of weed, ten keys of cocaine, ten thousand Ecstasy pills, ten thousand Morphine pills, twenty thousand Xanax pills, eight handguns, two Mack-11s, five fully automatic assault rifles, and what appeared to be at $25,000 to $40,000 in jewelry.

"So, how y'all wanna chop it up?" Chase asked.

"How 'bout this?" D-Mac suggested. "We split tha cash three ways. Since I don't slang dat girl no more, y'all can split tha ten bricks. Just let me have tha two hundred pounds of weed. As for tha pills, Osha can get tha X-pills, Chase will get tha Morphine, and I'll get tha bars. Y'all can split tha pistols and Mack-11s, and I'll take tha choppaz. Whateva y'all wanna do wit tha jewelry, dat's on y'all."

"That's what's up." Chase agreed.

"What we gon' do 'bout Bree?" Osha asked. "You know she gon' want somethin' for settin' this shit up."

"Did she saw when she was gon' hit you up?" D-Mac asked.

"Naw."

"Okay." Chase and Osha agreed.

"When she call you, give her my number, and have her to call me, and I'll meet her wit my portion." D-Mac suggested.

"A'ight."

After separating the take and distributing everyone's shares, they left and went their own separate ways.

RETRIBUTION&REVENGE**RETRIBUTION&REVENGE**RETRIBUTION&REVENGE

It was nearly ten o'clock when D-Mac arrived back at his room, where Rayne had been impatiently waiting.

"What's up?" D-Mac asked her, as he walked in the door. "What's goin' on?"

"I don't know. You tell me!" she scolded. "I tried to call your cell, but guess what? It was right here in tha nightstand! Then, you leave me here, by myself, talkin' 'bout you'll be back later, only it's twelve hours later! Where have you been and what have you done?!"

"Look." He responded, as he tossed two large, black trash bags on the bed. "Since this shit happened yesterday, I been wonderin' about some thangs."

"Like what?" she asked nervously.

"When I first started gettin' at you, I asked you if you was fuckin' wit somebody else, and you said you wasn't." He began. "That wasn't true, was it?"

"Baby, where is this coming from?"

"When I told Letha and them what Kevin said about you movin' dat pack for him and Lil' Paul, you didn't even deny it." He explained. "Dat could only mean one thang: you was still workin' for 'em when we was talkin', and you probably took 'em some shit after I got out, before you got fired!"

"No baby!" she pleaded, with tears in her eyes. "I stopped after I decided to be with you! That was before you even went up for parole!"

"You're lyin'!"

"No, I'm..."

"Bullshit!" he interrupted. "If you had stopped before then, they would've tried to take me out right then! They wouldn't wait till we hit tha streets, 'cause it's too risky. You lied to me, and it coulda got me and my sister killed!"

"Baby, I'm sor..."

"I'm not finished!" he yelled. "If you lied about dat, I wonder what else you lied about! I told you from tha beginnin' that I hate it when people lie to me, and if we gon' be together, I won't tolerate it from you! I even gave you tha opportunity to come clean and confess any lies you told me, wit no repercussions! What?! You didn't thank I would find out about it?!"

"I'm sorry baby." She said, as she began to cry. "I didn't think he would do nothing like this! I love you and I'm sorry!"

"If you loved me, you wouldn't have lied to me!" he snapped back at her. "I been doin' time wit Lil' Paul for years, and I know for a fact dat if he gotta bitch movin' dat sack for him, he fuckin' her too, right?!"

"Baby, please!" she pleaded. "It was all bus…"

"Business?!" he yelled. "So, it was business?! Since you like to sell pussy, let's put yo ass to work then! How 'bout dat?!"

"It's not like that!"

"Whateva." He laughed. "Gimme tha keys to both yo cars, and tha house. You can keep tha money in yo account. Use dat to take yo triflin' ass back to Clifton! Oh, yeah! Gimme those rings too!"

"Wait a minute baby!" she pleaded, realizing that her world was unraveling at an alarming rate. "Why don't you think about this before you make any rash decisions?"

"Think about it?!" he asked, sarcastically. "Tha only thang I need to thank about, is dat yo lyin' nearly got me and my sister killed! It ain't enough thankin' or forgiveness on this planet to get ova dat!"

"I'm sorry baby." She cried.

"Whateva. Put those keys and rangs on tha dresser. I'm finna take a shower, then I'm outta here."

While he was in the shower, D-Mac's phone rang.

"Hello?" Rayne answered.

"Is D-Mac there?" a female asked.

"He's in tha shower. Who is this?" Rayne asked, with a little hostility in her voice.

"This Bree." She responded. "Osha told me to holla at him 'bout some business."

"Can he reach you at this number?"

"Yeah."

"I'll tell him to call you when he gets out of the shower."

"Okay. Thanks."

"No problem."

Rayne hung up the phone, just as D-Mac came out of the shower.

"Who is Bree?" she asked.

"Dat's Osha's gal." he responded. "Did she call?"

"Yeah! What business is she talking about?"

"First of all, it's nothin' dat concerns you." He told her. "Second of all, don't touch my phone no more. You lost tha privilege to do that."

He picked up the phone and called Bree.

"Hello?"

"This Bree?"

"Yeah. Who is this?"

"This D-Mac."

"Hey! Osha told me to hit you up, 'cause you had somethin' for me."

"Yeah." He replied. "Where can we meet?"

"Where you at?"

"Near Opry Mills."

"Can you meet me out East?"

"Yeah. Anywhere in particular?"

"How 'bout tha Kroger on Dickerson Road at Ewing Lane?"

"A'ight." He agreed. "I'll call you when I get there."

After hanging up, D-Mac took $10,000 cash and placed it in an envelope. He then packed his clothes, and placed them, along with the trash bags from the robbery, into the trunk of his

Roadmaster. He grabbed both his and Rayne's keys, along with her wedding and engagement rings, and headed for the door.

"Baby, can we please just talk about this? Please?" she cried.

Without even saying a word, or glancing in her direction, D-Mac walked out of the door, and permanently out of Rayne's life.

RETRIBUTION&REVENGE**RETRIBUTION&REVENGE**RETRIBUTION&REVENGE

D-Mac called Bree as he pulled into the Kroger parking lot.

"Where you at?" he asked.

"I'm down tha street. I'll be there in a coupla minutes."

"Okay." He responded. "When you get here, go to tha eggs and milk aisle. I'm in all black, and I'll have a hand-held basket."

"A'ight. I'll have on a green t-shirt and some tan shorts."

D-Mac proceeded into the store to wait on Bree. He grabbed a hand-held basket, and half-filled it with miscellaneous items, before proceeding to the designated aisle. He appeared to be comparing prices when he saw Bree turn the corner.

He reached under his shirt and pulled out the envelope containing the money. As he passed her, he slipped the envelope into her hand and kept walking, He dropped the basket off at an empty register, then proceeded out the door and to his car.

As he pulled out of the parking lot, he placed a call.

"Hello?"

"What's goin' on gorgeous?" he asked.

"I'm surprised to be hearing from you! Where's Rayne?"

"She at tha hotel, and outta my life!"

"What happened?" Shannon asked.

"Well, I confronted her about what Kevin told me about her." He explained.

"What she have to say about it?"

"How about I come over and tell you about it?" he suggested.

"Where are you?"

"Out East."

"My address is 1105 Lischey Avenue."

"Okay. I'm on my way."

"Call me if you get lost." She teased.

"Will do."

When he arrived, D-Mac filled Shannon in over drinks and pizza. After a brief discussion of the forthcoming meeting with the Assistant District Attorney, they both decided to turn in for the night. Unfortunately, D-Mac couldn't get to sleep, because he couldn't stop thinking about the upcoming meeting.

Monday, April 13, 2009

D-Mac arrived at the Birch Building in downtown Nashville at 9 o'clock, for the appointment between the Assistant District Attorney and his "Dream Team" of defense counsels.

"So, what are you trying to do?" Assistant District Attorney, Jason Rutherford asked.

"I'm lookin' to have all charges dismissed, due to lack of evidence." D-Mac offered.

"We have several corroborating witness statements." He responded. "They all place you at the scene at the time of the shooting. They all place two weapons in your hands. They all identified you, from a photo line-up, as the shooter."

"I'ma need to look at those statements." D-Mac demanded.

"I don't know about that." Rutherford responded.

"So, what? You gon' make me wait until I file a Motion for Discovery in tha court?"

"I see you've been through this before."

"Actually, I'ma CLA."

"A what?"

"CLA. Certified Legal Assistant, or Paralegal. Whichever you prefer to call it."

"And the two of you are?" Rutherford asked, motioning towards Letha and Jennifer.

"They are part of my defense team from Memphis. Letha Latham, and Jennifer Echols."

"I'll tell you what. Give me a minute, and I'll get copies of the statements for you."

"Fine." D-Mac responded. "I'd also like copies of the photo line-ups you used, as well as all police reports pertaining to the shooting."

When he returned with copies of the requested documents, he handed them over to D-Mac, so that he could review them with his defense team.

"Do you mind?" he asked, when he saw that Rutherford had no intention of leaving.

"Sure." He replied, before finally turning to leave.

After reviewing the witness statements, police reports, and photo line-ups, they began comparing their notes.

"First of all," D-Mac began. "We gon' have to get tha ID tossed."

"How?" Shannon asked.

"You don't see tha issue wit these photos?"

"Spit it out!" Jennifer urged him.

"Tha otha guys' photos are from tha Davidson County Sheriff's Office. Notice tha orange jumpsuits? Mine, on tha otha hand, is a 2-0-1 photo." He explained. "It ain't hard to put two-and-two together wit dat. Shelby County tags and a Shelby County bookin' photo?"

"Okay." Letha adduced. "That shows deliberate and obvious prejudice, which taints the identification."

"How about out of nine witnesses, two said you had assault rifles, three said you had baby uzis, one said you had a black pistol, and three said you had a chrome pistol." Jennifer added.

"Anything else?" D-Mac asked.

"Yeah." Shannon began. "The police reports say the CID guys recovered sixty spent shell casings. But the witnesses all report hearing between fifteen and twenty-five shots."

"Hell, dat's a long way from sixty." D-Mac responded. "Anything else?"

"Well, there's an issue with your car." Letha added.

"What issue?"

"You gotta Lexus, right?"

"Yeah."

"Well, from the nine statements, you're driving anything from a Toyota Avalon, to an Infiniti Q45, to a Hyundai Sonata."

"What about tha tags?"

"Five gave a tag number, but none of them gave the *actual* tag number." Shannon spoke up. "The only thing they did get right, was that they were Shelby County plates."

"Then, the physical descriptions of the shooter were also off." Jennifer added. "They couldn't decide between dreads, braids, or waves."

"And," Shannon offered. "You're between 5'3" and 6'1" in height."

"Not to mention," Letha joined in. "You're brown-skinned and yellow."

"Okay. Let's call tha A.D.A. back in here and fuck his case off."

When Rutherford returned, D-Mac laid it all out.

"Look," he began. "There's so many holes in those statements, you could fly a space shuttle through them muthafuckaz! None of yo so-called witnesses positively identified my vehicle, nor did they supply an accurate plate number. The physical descriptions were way off, from my height, to my complexion, to my hair."

"That doesn't mean you're going to get me to dismiss the charges." Rutherford retorted.

"Oh, I ain't nowhere near done!" D-Mac snapped back. "According to tha statements, I had enough guns to go to war wit tha police. Not to mention dat bogus-ass line-up y'all used."

"There's nothing wrong with the line-ups!"

"It ain't? How about they were all Davidson County booking photos, except for mine, which just happened to be from Shelby County? You don't see nothin' wrong wit that?"

"What does that have to do with anything?"

"Tha fact that tha majority of tha witnesses reported seein' Shelby County tags, who do you think they'll choose in a line-up like dat? It's biased, and it's bullshit!"

"But…"

"Don't worry about it!" D-Mac interrupted. "We'll be preparing and filing a Motion to Suppress tha photo line-ups. Without that, you ain't got shit! No ID, no weapons, no tangible proof, only some bullshit statements. Period!"

With that being said, D-Mac, Letha, Jennifer and Shannon stood up and left the office.

"Crushed him." D-Mac said, more to himself, than anyone else. "Crushed him like a fuckin' roach."

"Let's go celebrate, then we can prep those motions for the Grand Jury hearing." Letha suggested.

"Anywhere special y'all wanna go?" D-Mac asked.

"How 'bout Princess' Fried Chicken out East?" Shannon recommended.

"On Ewing Lane?" D-Mac asked.

"Yeah."

"Let's go."

They all climbed in their cars and headed out to celebrate their small, victory.

RETRIBUTION&REVENGE**RETRIBUTION&REVENGE**RETRIBUTION&REVENGE

"So, what's next?" Jennifer asked, when they arrived at Shannon's house to begin the preparations.

"All we can do is wait it out." Shannon answered.

"But, in case dat don't work, we need to go 'head and figga out what we gon' do next." D-Mac added. "I don't wanna get blindsided, or as they say, 'get caught wit my pants down'. Feel me?"

"If the Grand Jury comes back with a True Bill, what kind of offer will you consider taking?" Shannon asked.

"Wait a minute." Letha intervened. "Evidently, you don't know my cousin too well."

"What do you mean?"

"He's not taking any kind of plea agreement."

"Is that so?" she asked, looking at D-Mac.

"Did you even look into tha case that got me on parole in tha first place?" he asked.

"Well, you're on parole from a twenty-year sentence for Voluntary Manslaughter, Felon in Possession of a Firearm, and two counts of Reckless Endangerment." She answered. "And that's at thirty-five percent."

"And how did I receive those charges and dat time?"

"Well, considering you was indicted for First-Degree Murder and two counts of Attempted First-Degree Murder," she recited. "I assumed you had pled out to the lesser offenses."

"Really? Well," D-Mac mocked her. "You assumed wrong beautiful. A jury found me guilty of tha lesser offenses, after being given instructions listing them as lesser-included offenses."

"I guess I didn't research thoroughly enough."

"Also, are you familiar with why I did what I did?"

"No."

"Tha nigga he killed had jumped on his little sister." Letha explained. "Tha otha two niggaz tried to jump him when he walked in tha house."

"Whose house was it?" Shannon asked.

"My sister's." D-Mac responded. "She called me when tha nigga put his hands on her. I don't play that shit!"

"Okay. You know tha D.A. is going to bring that up, right?"

"Yeah. But if I get my sister to testify about what happened, will dat help?"

"It depends on what happened, exactly." She explained. "Did you not have any other choice?"

"When I walked in her bedroom, he was standin' over her wit a butcha knife." He told her, with a hint of aggression. "If I didn't kill *him*, he woulda killed *her*!"

"Who else can we call as character witnesses, to show that you're not the animal they're trying to portray you to be?"

"There's James and Mashiek, who rents one of my houses in Cordova." He offered. "There's Rodger and Clara renting tha otha house I got in Cordova, Lamont and Charlinda, rentin' anotha one in Millington, J.T. and Althea rentin'-to-own one in Germantown, Jackie and Sonya renting one in Collierville, Edward and Melanie renting one in Arlington, and Trivonna rentin' a duplex in Orange Mound."

"Anyone who works with you or for you?"

"There's tha guys I hired to make any and all repairs dat needs to be made on my properties." He replied. "What good can they do?"

"They can offer an idea as to what type of person you are to work for."

"Well, Quantae and Trè are in charge of tha Cordova properties, Antonio's in charge of Millington, Eugene is in charge of

Collierville, Tony in Arlington, then Michael and Maurice in Orange Mound."

"How much do you pay them?"

"What does it matter?"

"Character!" she exclaimed. "If you pay them a decent wage or salary, and offer any type of benefits, then you can't possibly be the type of person they're portraying you to be."

"I pay 'em $600 a week to be on call, then, they get an additional fee which depends on tha job." He explained. "They get holidays off unless an emergency situation arises that can't wait. If that's tha case, I'll even go wit 'em to help, if I don't do tha entire job myself. I give 'em two weeks paid vacation time for tha summer. Spring also, if they have children.

"I even offer to file their tax returns for 'em, free of charge, if they need it. Then, if I buy anotha property, I'll pay 'em between $1,200 and $2,500 for minor renovations and repairs, depending on what needs to be done. I also buy tha supplies they need for each job."

"Any type of health or medical coverage?"

"I gottem all covered under my company policy with State Farm. It includes medical, dental, and vision, not only for them, but for their families too."

"Wow! Maybe I need to come work for you, just for the medical." Shannon teased.

"So, what do you want to start filing?" Jennifer asked.

"Let's start with a Motion for Discovery." D-Mac said. "Then, we'll file a Motion to Suppress tha photo line-ups they used."

"What about tha witness statements?" Letha asked.

"We need to conduct full and thorough background checks on all of tha witnesses." He answered. "I wanna know everything from parkin' tickets to felonies." If they mama in tha system, I wanna know about dat too!"

"What kind of defense do you want to use in general?" Shannon asked.

"A biased line-up resulting in prejudicial and unreliable identification." He responded. "All tha witness statements contradict each otha. Tha weapons described range from pistols to choppaz, and tha vehicle descriptions were completely off point. None of 'em even mentioned seein' a Lexus, and none of 'em gave an accurate tag number, otha than tha fact I got Shelby County plates."

"You know what?" Letha interrupted. "How did they even get a description of your car with the tag number in the first place, if none of the witnesses came close?"

"You right." D-Mac concurred. "Tha closest description they had, I believe, was a Toyota Avalon, but it's neither tha right make nor model. It's close, because they built on tha same platform. We need to find out how they ended up wit my tag number."

"Anything else?" Shannon asked.

"Tha physical descriptions in all tha statements contradict each otha. As a matter of fact, we can use 'em to rip they case apart."

"How can we use 'em?" Jennifer asked.

"The Sixth Amendment gives me the right to confront the witnesses and accusers the State are going to use against me, right?" D-Mac asked.

"Yeah." Letha answered.

"Well, we'll have to put those witnesses on tha stand for either direct examination or cross-examination, if the State calls them." He explained. "When they get on tha stand, we'll use that opportunity to show the discrepancies in their statements.

"After they all done testified, we can put the testimonies and statements together, and show that they couldn't have pinpointed me as a suspect. They have no prints on tha casin's, and they don't have tha murda weapon or weapons."

"So, if we get tha line-up tossed, and discredit the witnesses, we'll basically destroy the State's case!" Letha articulated. "Let's do it!"

"Alright." D-Mac said, as he stood up. "It's almost 6 o'clock, and I got some thangs I need to tend to. So, let's finish this up tomorrow."

"Dat's what's up." Letha replied.

She and Jennifer gathered their copies of documents, their notes, and headed back to their hotel room.

RETRIBUTION&REVENGE**RETRIBUTION&REVENGE**RETRIBUTION&REVENGE

"Now that we finally have some alone time." Shannon said, as she threw her arms around D-Mac's neck. "What are we going to do with it?"

"You look like you kinda sick baby girl."

"Well, now that you mention it, I haven't been feeling too good Daddy."

"What would make you feel better baby?"

"Some of that sexual healing you have for me." She said, with a seductive smile.

"It's time for me to heal you then."

He picked her up and carried her to the bedroom, where he gently laid her down, as he planted sensual kisses on her luscious lips. The passion between them immediately began to manifest itself in radiant warmth and spontaneous impulses, which would drive the average individual to the brink of clinical insanity.

"Can I ask you somethin' beautiful?" he asked.

"Sure. What is it?"

"When was tha last time you had a man to make, slow, passionate love to you?"

"Wow!" she exclaimed. "Where is this coming from?"

"I'm just wonderin'."

"Well," she paused in contemplation. "It's actually been so long ago, that I can't even remember."

"How 'bout I give you a reminder as to how it feels?" he smiled.

"I'd love that."

D-Mac slowly slid himself inside of her warm, wet and throbbing sanctuary. She moaned slightly as he pushed further in, gently with each stroke, going deeper and deeper. He kissed her softly, yet with tremendous passion. Her body moved in simultaneous rhythm with his. Their movement, their breathing, their heartbeats became as one.

She wrapped her legs around his waist, looked deep into his eyes, and dug her nails into his back, as he seemed to go deeper and deeper within her inner being. They gradually increased their momentum as one, but when he began to feel Shannon's body tense and her muscles contract, he made them both slow their pace in order to lengthen the experience.

"Oh, baby!" Shannon cried out. "Please, don't make me wait!"

"Trust me. It'll be worth it baby." He assured her.

She tightened her legs around his waist, and arched her back, in anticipation of the long-awaited and forthcoming explosion. But, not wanting to wait any longer, she decided to take control of the situation.

She rolled him off of her, and mounted him before he could even react. She leaned down to kiss him, as she began to bounce on his dick. Up and down, harder and harder, faster and faster. As she began to feel the climax approaching, she rose up, and increased the intensity of her movements. D-Mac moved his hips in sync with hers.

"Oh yes! Daddy, that's it!" Shannon yelled out. "Give it to me Daddy! Oh shit! I'm comin' Daddy! I'm comin'!"

At that moment, they both exploded into pure, unrestrained ecstasy. She laid her head on his chest, as he wrapped his arms around her, and there they remained, with him still inside of her. She listened intently, and realized that their hearts continued to beat as one.

"I've never experienced that before."

"What's that?" he asked.

"You made me feel special." She began explaining. "You weren't just trying to get yours, but you wanted us to get ours together. Plus, I noticed that both our hearts and our breathing was on one accord during that experience, and they remain so, even now."

"So, what are you tryna say?" he asked.

"I've been searching for that feeling for fifteen years or so. No one, and I mean no one, has made love to me the way you just did, making me feel the way I now feel."

"And how do you feel?"

"When you was making love to me, I felt as though there was something more than just the sexual satisfaction. You made me feel wanted, appreciated. Most of all, you made me feel loved. And…"

"What is it?" he attempted to coax her to continue. "I made you feel loved and what?"

"If I tell you, you'll probably think I'm krazie." She laughed.

"Try me." He encouraged her, as he locked onto her deep, brown eyes.

"I think I've fallen in love…with you."

D-Mac maintained eye contact as he processed what he had just heard.

"Are you sure?"

"Yes. I mean, I believe so." She struggled, attempting to find the right way to express the way he was making her feel "It's so different, the feelings I'm having. They're so different and unexpected. I've never experienced this before, so it could only be one thing…love."

"So, where do you wanna go from here?" he asked her.

"I want you to move in with me, at least until after the trial." She told him. "If it works out between us, will you be willing to sell your house in Memphis and stay with me permanently?"

"Sell my house?!" he laughed. "Absolutely not! But I'll move in with you, and if it works out, I'll just put my house on the market for rent."

"That's fine with me!" she said with a smile, as she kissed him.

There they remained, falling asleep in each other's arms, with him still inside of her.

Tuesday, April 14, 2009

"Davidson County District Attorney's Office, how may I direct your call?"

"May I speak with Jason Rutherford, please?"

"He's not available right now. May I take a message, and have him to call you back?"

"Sure. My name is Rayne Morgan-Franklin, and he can reach me at 901-229-8948."

"And may I ask what it's concerning?"

"Tell him I have some information on the double homicide involving Derrick Franklin."

"Okay. I'll have him call you as soon as he gets in."

"Thank you."

"You're welcome."

Unbeknownst to Rayne, she had made a critical mistake. One that could potentially cost her the one thing that she might not be able to save: her life.

RETRIBUTION&REVENGE**RETRIBUTION&REVENGE**RETRIBUTION&REVENGE

"Are you sure?"

"I'm positive. She just called, and I have her message right her in my hand. Good thing you told me you were representing him."

"Okay. Thanks sis. I'll let him know."

Shannon returned to the bedroom and woke D-Mac from a peaceful sleep.

"Baby! Get up! It's important!"

"What's wrong?" he asked, as he sat up with a start.

"My sister Telisha just called. She said that Rayne just called the D.A.'s Office looking for Rutherford, and left a message that she had information on the case."

"Are you fuckin' serious?" he yelled, as he jumped up.

He grabbed his clothes and his phone, and then ran into the bathroom.

"I'ma kill dat bitch!" he yelled.

"No, you're not." Shannon told him. "I have a better idea. Let me make a few calls."

RETRIBUTION&REVENGE**RETRIBUTION&REVENGE**RETRIBUTION&REVENGE

Rayne was in the hotel room, heart thumping and mind racing. She knew that she was at fault for everything which had recently transpired with D-Mac, from the double homicides, to him walking out of her life. She also knew how strongly he hated rats, snitches and informants. As she contemplated this, she became terrified, and wondered if D-Mac would kill her if he found out, or rather *when* he found out.

She knew, deep down, that she was wrong for seeking revenge against him for leaving, when she caused it with her lying. As quickly as she thought it, she dismissed it just as quickly, and chalked it up as her having to do the right thing. Knowing what she had done, she wouldn't feel safe until he was back in prison, and right now, she was the only person who could give the District Attorney what he needed in order to secure a conviction against D-Mac.

Tears streamed down her face as it dawned on her. She was preparing to become the State's star witness against the man she so deeply loves. She also knew that as long as he was on the streets, she wouldn't be safe, and her life would be in jeopardy. She knew she would have to disappear. When the A.D.A. calls her back, she'll ask to be placed in protective custody, and possibly the witness protection program.

"You're doing what's right." She tried to reassure herself out loud. "He didn't have to kill 'em the way he did, and even so, he shouldn't have left me the way he did, knowing that I know what I know."

As she was talking to herself, there came a knock at the door.

"Who is it?" she called out.

"I'm Melanie Hawkins with the District Attorney's Office." A woman responded. "Rutherford told me to bring you downtown so he can formally take your statement."

As Rayne opened the door, three women rushed in, grabbing her, and forcing her to the floor. One of the women removed a strip of duct tape from her shirt and placed it firmly over her mouth to keep her from screaming. She heard the door close as they began to tie her hands and feet together.

She looked around and discovered that all three women wore sunglasses and hats, and had gloves hanging from their pockets. Her raced and her breathing quickened as she realized what *had* happened, what *was* happening, and what was *going* to happen. It didn't take a rocket scientist to realize that somehow, D-Mac had found out about her call to the District Attorney's Office, and had sent someone to silence her.

RETRIBUTION&REVENGE**RETRIBUTION&REVENGE**RETRIBUTION&REVENGE

The three women: Melanie Tate; Tameka Smith and Lauren Green, were clients of Shannon's. She had represented all three of them at one point or another, and since she had gotten them off, they all said that if she needed anything, just call.

Melanie Tate had been charged with Attempted 2nd Degree Murder, because she mercilessly beat her ex-boyfriend within inches of death with a baseball bat, because he had jumped on her. Because the police had taken her to the hospital prior to arresting her, and her injuries had been documented and photographed, the District Attorney decided to drop the charges. He knew that in light of the abuse she had suffered immediately prior to the assault, no jury in America would convict her.

Tameka Smith had been charged with Aggravated Robbery and Especially Aggravated Kidnapping. However, since kidnapping was essentially incidental to the robbery, Shannon convinced the Assistant District Attorney to dismiss that count of the indictment. Then, since she didn't possess or use a deadly weapon or anything fashioned as such, during the commission of the robbery, the A.D.A. extended a plea of simple robbery, with a sentence of three years of diversion probation. Once she completed the probation without incident, she was able to have the charge expunged from her record.

Lauren Green had been charged with 1st Degree Murder, for killing her then boyfriend, who had molested her four-year-old daughter. When she came home early from work one day, she caught him in the act, in the bedroom they shared, and retrieved the gun she kept in the drawer of her nightstand. She fired all thirteen rounds from the 9mm semi-automatic pistol into his chest. The A.D.A. was pushing for a trial, until Shannon revealed that they would be putting Lauren's then six-year-old daughter on the stand to testify. With that announcement, combined with the results of her daughter's rape kit, the intense publicity and the high-profile nature of the case, the A.D.A. wisely dismissed the charges, as she knew she would never be able to secure a conviction.

RETRIBUTION&REVENGERETRIBUTION&REVENGE**RETRIBUTION&REVENGE**

"We heard dat you like to snitch on muthafuckaz!" Lauren exclaimed. "What's up wit that shit?"

Rayne vigorously shook her head as she tried to speak through the tape, which had been placed over her mouth.

"Let's see what tha botch gotta say." Tameka suggested.

Lauren removed the tape as Melanie stepped into view, holding a small, black, semi-automatic pistol.

"Speak!" Lauren demanded.

"I'm sorry! I was scared, and didn't know what to do!" Rayne pleaded. "If you let me go, I won't say anything to anyone! I swear! Tell D-Mac I'm sorry, and I swear I won't say anything!"

Melanie motioned to Lauren, who put the tape back over Rayne's mouth.

"I don't know how they do shit where you from," Melanie began. "But 'round here, we deal with rats tha way they should be dealt with!"

She went and sat on the bed, then gave instructions to both Lauren and Tameka.

"Beat dat bitch!"

Smiles spread across their faces, as they pulled on their black gloves and began to viciously pummel Rayne, as she lay on the floor, unable to defend herself.

Rayne began to cry and pray as the blows kept coming, one after another, after another, after another. She tried to think about the happier moments she had shared with D-Mac, in an effort to take her mind off the pain. She then wondered how he could consciously order the brutal assault of the woman he once claimed to love. She immediately remembered that this is the same man who killed three individuals in cold blood, and those were just the ones she knew about. How many more had he killed, which had yet to surface?"

After what seemed like an eternity to Rayne, the blows ceased. She couldn't see, because both of her eyes were swollen shut. She had to breathe through her mouth, because they had obviously broken her nose. She felt pain all over her body. Her head felt as though it was three times its normal size. She thought to herself that if they were to leave, she'd go to the hospital, get treated, rent a car, and leave Tennessee forever.

She heard movement around her, and then suddenly, pain exploded first in her back, then in her chest. She realized that they had taken a short break, and had continued the brutal assault with vicious kicks. There was a loud cracking sound, followed by intense pain in her side. She knew they had just broken some ribs.

"Stop!" Melanie demanded, as she stood up and looked down on the viciously battered body. When she first entered the room, she could see why someone would want to marry Rayne, because she was both beautiful and sexy. Now, she looked nothing like her former self.

She knelt down beside Rayne and whispered in her ear.

"I know that if you were to survive this, you will *never* look the same, and you'd probably kill yourself. I would love to let you go just to see it, but I have my orders."

Rayne began to cry and tremble violently, as she knew, she had just received confirmation that she was not leaving that room alive.

Lauren removed a hypodermic needle from her pocket, which contained a massive dose of an intravenous blood thinner. She removed the cap and injected the triple dosage into Rayne's arm.

After she was done, Tameka removed a switchblade from her pocket and opened it. As she stepped towards Rayne, Melanie stopped her.

"Let me do tha honor." She said, as she took the knife from Tameka.

She stepped over to Rayne, and bending down, slit her throat deeply, from ear-to-ear. Blood spewed forth like an open faucet. She suddenly realized that she was actually enjoying this part a little too much.

After five minutes, Lauren checked for a pulse.

"She's gone."

Melanie removed the tape from Rayne's mouth, and began to gather anything that they had brought with them, while Lauren and Tameka untied her hands and feet. After double-checking the room, they walked out, leaving Rayne's lifeless and battered body in the room on the floor. As an afterthought, Tameka placed the "Do Not Disturb" sign on the room's outer door handle.

RETRIBUTION&REVENGE**RETRIBUTION&REVENGE**RETRIBUTION&REVENGE

D-Mac and Shannon were in Letha and Jennifer's room going over the case, when the call came in.

"I have to take this call, excuse me." Shannon said, as she went into the bathroom.

"It's done." Melanie told her, once she answered the phone.

"Thanks. How much do I owe y'all?"

"Nothin'. We're even." She responded. "If you need us again, give us a call."

"That's fine with me, but he's gonna want to give you something. That's just who he is."

"Whateva he feels is fair. Just as long as you're tha one who brings it."

"I'll bring him with me. You'll know him when you see him, but it has to be somewhere secluded."

"Where y'all at?" Melanie asked, after a brief silence.

"Out East. Brick Church Pike and Trinity Lane."

"Meet us at tha park on Old Hickory Boulevard, offa Dickerson Road."

"Okay. "We'll be in a champagne-colored Lexus."

"See you when we get there."

After disconnecting the call, Shannon called D-Mac into the bathroom.

"What's goin' on?" he asked.

"Tha problem with Rayne has been taken care of."

"Really?"

"Yeah. How much are you willing to pay the three individuals who handled it?"

"Did she just leave town, or is she gone permanently?"

"Permanently."

"I'll give 'em ten racks each. Where we meetin' 'em at?"

"Near Madison."

D-Mac stuck his head out the door, and told Letha to toss him his attaché case. In it, he had a laptop computer, writing pads, pens, and $50,000 in cash. He removed three bands of $10,000 each, and put them in his pockets.

"Let's go." He told Shannon.

RETRIBUTION&REVENGE**RETRIBUTION&REVENGE**RETRIBUTION&REVENGE

When they pulled into a shaded area of the parking lot and parked, they had been waiting only a few minutes before Melanie, Tameka, and Lauren appeared. D-Mac unlocked the doors and they all climbed into the back seat.

"Well, I'll be damned!" Lauren exclaimed.

"You know him?" Melanie asked.

"And you don't?" Tameka inquired. "That's Derrick Franklin! He tha one they say did that double murda in U.C. last week!"

"Really?" Melanie questioned.

"That's what they say anyway." D-Mac responded. "They don't have a sure-fire case. I basically told 'em to suit up, 'cause I'm takin' this shit to trial."

"Dat's what's up." Melanie told him. "What you got for us?"

D-Mac reached into his pockets, and removed the bundles of cash.

"Here's $10,000 each." He explained. "Once it hit tha news dat she ain't wit us no more, I'll give y'all anotha five racks each."

They all took their portions and began to climb out of the car, when D-Mac noticed someone taking photos of them from another car.

"Don't get out yet." He demanded.

"Why?" Melanie asked.

D-Mac reached under his seat and grabbed a baby Glock 9mm, equipped with a compact silencer.

"I'll be back." He said, as he tucked the pistol in his waist.

He got out of the car, while Shannon, Melanie, Tameka, and Lauren watched as he approached the other car.

"What you doin'?" he asked the man, when he reached the car.

"Nothin'."

"Lemme get dat camera partna."

"Fuck off!" the man responded, as he reached for the ignition.

D-Mac calmly looked around, as he pulled out the pistol, and shot the man twice in his left temple. He opened the door with his shirt tail, reached in, and grabbed the digital camera. He then turned and casually walked back to the Lexus.

"What tha hell D?!" Shannon exclaimed.

Without a word, he showed them the images in the camera.

"Why was he takin' pictures of us?" Tameka asked.

"Either he a reporter, or a private investigator. If he a private investigator, I'll bet ten-to-one, he was hired by Rutherford." He explained. "We'll know when it hit tha news."

With that being said, Melanie, Tameka, and Lauren climbed out of the Lexus, and D-Mac pulled off.

"Did you have to kill him?" Shannon asked.

"No witnesses baby." D-Mac responded. "We can't leave witnesses."

"But he didn't witness anything!"

"He witnessed us meeting with three women, who just so happened to be Rayne's killaz. If they happen to connect them to tha murda, then these photos surface, they won't hesitate to charge the both of us with Conspiracy to commit Murda One!" he explained.

"I didn't look at it like that." She admitted.

"Don't worry baby. We'll be okay." He assured her.

After grabbing something to eat, they went back to Shannon's house and waited. There was nothing on the 11 o'clock nor the 12 o'clock news, about Rayne's murder. The 5 o'clock news was another story altogether.

"Good evening. I'm Vicki Yates. We have some breaking news developing at the Opryland Hotel. At around three-thirty this afternoon, Metro police received a call from hotel management, that the housekeeping staff had discovered the body of a brutally beaten woman in one of their suites. Nicole Ferguson is on the scene with more information. What can you tell us Nicole?"

"Metro police has identified the victim through hotel records, as twenty-two-year-old Rayne Franklin. She's the wife of Derrick Franklin, who, if you'll recall, is the suspect in last week's double homicide in the University Court public housing projects, in South Nashville.

"Franklin had been viciously beaten beyond

recognition, and her throat had been slit. Police are interviewing hotel staff, to see if anyone saw anything. The Metro police spokesman had this to say…"

"We don't have any leads or suspects at this time. We're asking that if the public has heard or seen anything, to call Crime Stoppers at 74-CRIME. We're also searching for Derrick Franklin for questioning. He's not a suspect at this time, but we're hoping that maybe he can shed some light on the situation."

"Reporting Live from Opryland Hotel, I'm Nicole Ferguson, News Channel 5 HD. Vicki?"

"Derrick Franklin is currently free on a $150,000 bond, for the University Court homicides.

"Metro received yet another report of a body found in Cedar Park, on Old Hickory Boulevard, near Dickerson Road. The victim, identified as forty-one-year-old Justin Morris. In a coincidental twist, he had been assigned by the District Attorney's Office, to conduct surveillance on

Derrick Franklin. He was a free-lance private investigator, who was frequently hired by the D.A.'s Office. Police say that Morris had been shot multiple times in the head.

"This is the second incident that has somewhat circumstantial connections to Derrick Franklin, in less than a week following the double homicides in University Court. Police urge that anyone with any information regarding either of the three incidents, call Crime Stoppers.

"Earlier today ..."

D-Mac muted the television and picked up the phone.

"Who are you calling?" Shannon asked.

"Rutherford."

"Why?" she asked, concerned.

"It'll look suspicious if I don't." He explained.

"Davidson County District Attorney's Office, how may I direct your call?"

"Jason Rutherford."

"May I ask who's calling?"

"Derrick Franklin."

"I'll see if he's available."

The receptionist placed D-Mac on hold. After a few minutes, Assistant District Attorney, Jason Rutherford, was on the line.

"What can I do for you Mr. Franklin?" he asked.

"First of all, you could've had tha fuckin' decency to call me and let me know dat my wide had been murdered, instead of lettin' me find out through tha fuckin' evenin' news!" D-Mac demanded.

"Calm down, Mr. …"

"Don't tell me to fuckin' calm down!" D-Mac yelled. "Did you even notify her parents and family?"

"No. I didn't."

"So, chances are, they found out tha same way I did!"

"Are they from Nashville?" Rutherford asked, nervously.

"No! They from Clifton, but they watch tha Nashville news! Dat's just fuckin' great!"

"I tried to call you, but…"

"Bullshit! My phone is always on, and has been all day! There isn't a single call from your office! Don't play fuckin' games wit me right now, you egotistical bitch!"

"Hold on now...."

"Fuck dat! Not only did you not notify me nor her family before plastering her name and picture on tha news, but you basically insinuated dat I was somehow involved!"

"Wait a minute!" Rutherford jumped in. "That was Metro, not..."

"Yeah! It was Metro all right, workin' wit tha fuckin' D.A.'s Office! Don't forget, I'm smarter than you bitches give me credit for, you ig'nant-ass bitch! Then, you try to pin anotha murda on me, dat I had absolutely nothin' to do wit! Not to mention tha fact dat you illegally hired tha alleged victim to conduct surveillance on me!"

"Now, hold on..."

"Fuck you! Fuck tha D.A.'s Office! And fuck Metro! I'm filin' a Federal Complaint against all you muthafuckaz before tha week's out! Some jobs gone be lost and some careers ended! Now, shed some light on dat! You arrogant sons of bitches!"

Before Rutherford could get another word in, D-Mac had hung up on him.

"Damn! Shannon exclaimed.

"What?"

"I've never heard *anyone* talk to Rutherford like that!" she said.

"I had to make it believable." He smiled.

RETRIBUTION&REVENGE**RETRIBUTION&REVENGE**RETRIBUTION&REVENGE

"What in the hell did you do John?" Rutherford asked Metro spokesman, John Barron.

"What?"

"You released his wife's name and photo to the media, without notifying him?"

"It's possible that he had something to do with her murder."

"But still," Rutherford said, rubbing his temples. "Even so, you didn't even notify her parents, who just happens to live here in Middle Tennessee, and watches our local news reports."

"It's not that bad. I'll take responsibility for that." Barron assured him.

"That's not all." Rutherford continued. "You told them that I assigned Morris to conduct surveillance on Franklin?"

"So! What's wrong with that?"

"So?" Rutherford growled. "So?! I didn't obtain a warrant to authorize the surveillance! That's a Constitutional violation, not to mention, prosecutorial misconduct! He's coming after my fucking job!"

"How can you be sure he'll think like that?"

"You don't know, do you?"

"Know what?" Barron asked, nervously.

"I looked him up." Rutherford said, as he began typing on his keyboard. "Look!" he said, as he turned the screen for Barron to see.

"Oh shit." Barron said, as he read what was on the screen.

"Exactly!" Rutherford replied. "He's a Certified Legal Assistant, specializing in Criminal Law; Civil Litigation; Contractual Law; Corporate Law; and Constitutional Law. He knows his shit, and knows how to use it."

"How good is he?"

"At his arraignment, I requested tha he be remanded. On his own, he argued the Judge down from remand, to $2 Million, to a $150,000 bond, which he immediately made, with no problem. Then," he continued. "He single-handedly poked holes in the entire case so far, during our first meeting. I'm talking holes so big, you can fly a space shuttle through it."

"What should we do?"

"I don't know about you, but I'm going to prepare my letter of resignation."

"Why?"

"You heard him!" Rutherford exclaimed. "He clearly said 'some jobs are gonna be lost and some careers ended!' I'd rather resign and keep my pension, than get fired and lost it."

"So, you're not going to fight him?"

"I'm going to fight him, but when he files that Federal Complaint, I'm going to submit my resignation just in case. If I beat him, then I'll be able to come back. Otherwise, no harm, no foul."

"If you resign, you're giving him what he wants." Barron tried to reason.

"Maybe so, but you gave him the ammunition he needed in your press releases and statements."

RETRIBUTION&REVENGE**RETRIBUTION&REVENGE**RETRIBUTION&REVENGE

After ending the call with Rutherford, D-Mac called Rayne's parents, who had indeed watched the report of their daughter's murder. After succeeding in assuring them that he had absolutely nothing to do with her murder, he told them of his plans to file a Federal Complaint, and asked if they wanted to be named as Plaintiffs. They declined, and said that no amount of money would bring their daughter back.

Throughout the night, and throughout the early hours of the following morning, D-Mac and Shannon worked overtime, researching and preparing, a 42 U.S.C. § 1983 Civil Complaint against Assistant District Attorney, Jason Rutherford, and Metro Police spokesman John Barron, among other individuals.

Wednesday, April 15, 2009

After typing and printing off the final draft of the Federal Complaint, D-Mac, along with Shannon, Letha, and Jennifer, pulled up to the United States Courthouse, amid a frenzied crowd of local and national news reporters.

D-Mac had made several calls and sent several emails early that morning to multiple media outlets, letting them know that he and his defense team would be holding a press conference in front of the United States Courthouse on Broadway, in downtown Nashville, at 9 o'clock. He also attached to each email, a copy of the Federal Complaint he had prepared, which he would file immediately following the press conference.

As they approached the bank of microphones, they waited for the anxious crowd to quiet down before they began, starting with the introductions.

"Good morning," Shannon began. "I'm Shannon Swift of Nashville, and I'm lead counsel in Derrick Franklin's defense team. Serving as co-counsels are Letha Latham and Jennifer Echols, both from Memphis. Also assisting, as a Certified Legal Assistant, or Paralegal, is Derrick Franklin himself."

There arose a lot of murmurs and whispers at the announcement of D-Mac's certification as a Paralegal, and that he would be assisting in his own defense.

"I'll now present to you the person who called this press conference; Mr. Derrick Franklin." Shannon finished.

D-Mac stepped up to the bank of microphones and waited for the crowd to simmer down once again, before he started to speak.

"Good morning!" he began. "As I'm sure you're all aware, there was a double homicide which occurred in University Court this past Saturday, for which I have been wrongly accused and charged. However, that's not tha reason for this press conference. The true reason for this conference is the occurrence of multiple incidents yesterday, which culminated in the slanging of false accusations and in indirect confession of Constitutional violations, via tha local media.

"First of all, my wife, Rayne Franklin, who's originally from Clifton, Tennessee, was violently murdered in our hotel suite at tha Opryland Hotel where we were staying. Neither I, nor her family, were notified of her death, nor were we given an opportunity to positively identify her body, before her name, photograph, and details of her gruesome murder were released to the media for broadcasting and publication, by Metro spokesman John Barron.

To add insult to injury, he publicly stated, that I was being sought for questioning concerning her murder, adding that I could maybe 'shed some light on the situation.' That statement, in and of itself, possessed a strong sense of insinuation, that I somehow could have been involved in her murder, which is absolutely and positively ridiculous.

"If that statement was as innocent as he'll more than likely try to make it seem later, then all he had to do was pick up the phone and dial my number, or contact my attorneys, whose numbers I'm certain he has on hand. However, he didn't bother to do that, in order to notify me of my wife's murder, nor to notify me that I was wanted for questioning.

"Secondly, according to media reports, a private investigator was shot multiple times and murdered in Cedar Park, on Old Hickory Boulevard in Madison. It had been revealed, through an authorized press release, that this investigator was assigned, allegedly, to conduct surveillance on me, at the direction of Assistant District Attorney, Jason Rutherford. After conducting a simple investigation of my own, I discovered that A.D.A. Rutherford never secured a warrant for such surveillance.

"That is a violation of the Fourth Amendment of the United States Constitution, which states that 'The right of the people to be secure in their persons, houses, papers, and effects, against unreasonable searches and seizures, shall not be violated, and no Warrants shall issue, but upon probable cause, supported by oath or affirmation,…' By illegally using government funds to authorize and sanction surveillance, without the issuance of a warrant to do so, and without any probable cause, A.D.A. Rutherford is not only guilty of violating the Fourth Amendment's prohibition against Illegal Search and Seizure, but he's also guilty of prosecutorial misconduct.

"He and Metro spokesman, John Barron, are also guilty of defamation and slander, as it pertains to the insinuations of me being involved in my wife's murder.

"In addition to filing *this* Federal Complaint," he stated, while holding up a copy for all to see. "I'm also filing a Temporary Restraining Order, which is asking the assigned Judge to issue an Order preventing both Jason Rutherford and John Barron from resigning, until after the disposition of this case.

"I'm also filing a request for Preliminary Injunction, which is asking that they both be suspended from their jobs without pay, pending the disposition of this case. As part of my prayer for relief, I'm asking that they both be terminated from their jobs; that Jason Rutherford be barred from holding any public judicial office; that Jason Rutherford's license to practice law be permanently revoked; and that John Barron be barred from obtaining *any* employment that's even *remotely* connected to law enforcement, to include, but is not limited to, unarmed security.

"I have forwarded a copy of this Complaint, along with all attachments, to your respective offices, via email. Now, if you'll excuse me, myself, accompanied by my defense team, will now enter the United States Courthouse and file these documents in the United States District Court for the Middle District of Tennessee at Nashville, with the Office of the Clerk. Thank you all for your time and attention."

After concluding the press conference, D-Mac, Shannon, Letha and Jennifer, all entered the United States Courthouse, and approached the Court Clerk's Office, where he submitted his Federal Complaint, along with the attachments, and paid the required filing fee, in cash.

After date and time stamping the Formal Complaint, the Temporary Restraining Order, and the Requests for Preliminary Injunction, the Clerk made a copy and handed it to D-Mac. They were surprised to see that the media was still in place when they exited the Courthouse. D-Mac took this moment to make one final announcement.

"The Complaint and accompanying documents have just been filed with the United States District Court Clerk's Office." He then leaned forward and stated: "Mr. Rutherford, Mr. Barron, your days of corruption, conspiracy and official misconduct, has officially come to an end, thanks to Derrick Franklin, CLA!"

With that being said, D-Mac and Shannon climbed into his Lexus, as Letha and Jennifer climbed into Letha's 2008 Nissan Maxima, and they drove off.

"My fuckin' career and pension is over." Rutherford said out loud, to an empty office, after seeing D-Mac's live press conference.

As he sat there at his desk, wondering what his next move would be, someone knocked at his door.

"Come in!" he called out.

His secretary opened the door, and stuck her head in slightly.

"Mr. Rutledge would like a word with you in his office." She told him.

"Tell him I'll be right there."

"Yes sir."

Samuel Rutledge was the Attorney General and Reporter for the State of Tennessee, which made him Rutherford's direct supervisor. The only person above him was the Governor of Tennessee.

"You wanted to see me, sir?" Rutherford asked, as he reluctantly entered the office.

"I take it that you saw Mr. Franklin's press conference this morning." Rutledge stated.

"I did."

"Not long after the filing of those documents, I received a call, not only from Federal Judge Chris Lawrence, but I also received a call from Mayor William Garrison. The mayor wanted me to put you on administrative leave with pay, but Judge Lawrence was obviously convinced by whatever Franklin placed in the Complaint, because he gave me a heads up that tomorrow morning, following a hearing, he would have no choice but to grant Franklin's Request for a Preliminary Injunction, that you be suspended without pay, pending the outcome of the case.

"He went on to say that if you want to avoid such suspension, that you had better present a damn good defense as to why he shouldn't grant the injunction."

"Excuse me, Mr. Rutledge," his secretary interrupted. "But there's a deputy here from the U. S. Marshall's Office looking for Mr. Rutherford."

"Damn! That was quick!" Rutledge exclaimed. "He must've had the damned Summons attached to the Complaint when he filed it. Send him in Clarissa."

A United States Marshall entered the room, with a brown manila envelope, and a clip board.

"Mr. Jason Rutherford?"

"Yes?"

"Would you sign here please?"

After Rutherford signed the form affixed to the clipboard, the Marshall made a few notations, and then handed the letter-sized manila envelope to Rutherford.

"You've just been served sir." The Marshall informed him, before leaving.

"Look," Rutledge began. "There's nothing else you can do today. Why don't you just go home, get some rest, and prepare for the hearing tomorrow?"

"Thank you, sir." Rutherford responded, as he left Rutledge's office.

A similar scenario played out in another nearby office building. This scenario, however, occurred between the Chief of Police, Howard Wilson, and Metro Spokesman, John Barron.

Chief Wilson received the same courtesy calls from both Judge Lawrence and Mayor Garrison. And just like Rutherford, Barron was served with his copy of the Complaint and its attachments.

Little did everyone know, this was just the beginning of a storm, which was about to spiral out of control, while being covered by national news media, the likes of *CNN*; *Good Morning America*; and the *Today Show*. All eyes would soon be on Nashville, and it will have nothing to do with Country Music; the Grand Ol' Opry, nor the Tennessee Titans.

RETRIBUTION&REVENGE**RETRIBUTION&REVENGE**RETRIBUTION&REVENGE

As they were gathered in Letha and Jennifer's hotel room, Shannon's phone chirped, notifying her that she had an email.

"Well, that was quick!" she said, after checking her email.

"What's that?" D-Mac asked.

"It's an email from the U.S. District Court Clerk's Office." She explained. "A hearing has been set regarding the TRO and the Preliminary Injunction, for tomorrow morning at 9 o'clock."

"Dat's what's up! Those bitches will be out of a job by noon!"

"What do you want to work on first?"

"They sealed their own fates in this case, so I'm not worried. Let's work on trying to prepare for the preliminary hearing on these mudras, and once we get that done, we can push for them to place the preliminary hearing on the earliest docket. If we beat 'em and get a dismissal, that'll be great, but we also gotta prepare for tha worst."

"Which is?"

"That they decide to bind the charges over to tha Grand Jury. If they do that and they come back with a True Bill, then we'll need to file a Motion for Fast and Speedy Trial. At tha beginning of tha trial, we need to be prepared to go at 'e, with everything. I don't wanna stone left unturned. When it's all said and done, I want either a Judgment of Acquittal from tha Judge, or a Not Guilty verdict from tha Jury."

"We have a lot of work ahead of us." Shannon sighed. "A *lot* of work."

The four of them debated, discussed, suggested, recommended and argued over different points, angles and methods to utilize at the forthcoming preliminary hearing, until well past 1 o'clock in the morning.

"We betta head out so we all can get some rest." D-Mac said, as he stood up to stretch. "We need to be refreshed for tomorrow's hearing in Federal Court."

He and Shannon said their goodbyes and headed back to her place for the night. Of course, D-Mac couldn't sleep, because he was so anxious to see what excuses Rutherford and Barron would attempt to use, in order to keep themselves from getting suspended, without pay, pending the disposition of the case.

Tuesday, April 16, 2009

"D-Mac! Come here, quick!" Shannon called out from the bedroom. "You're not going to believe this shit!"

When D-Mac came out of the bathroom, he directed his attention to the television. Holding a press conference of their own, were Assistant District Attorney Jason Rutherford, and Metro Police Spokesman John Barron.

"This is just a clever ploy by Derrick Franklin to avoid his impending convictions for the double homicide in University Court this past Saturday." Rutherford ranted. "He escaped a heavy prison sentence for a cold-blooded murder he committed in Memphis in 2000, in addition to two attempted murders. He ended up only receiving a twenty-year sentence, for which he's currently on parole, instead of a much-deserved life sentence, or better yet, the death penalty.

"These guys from Memphis and other big crime cities think that they can come to Nashville, kill our residents, and get away with it, using poorly disguised tactics such as those being deployed by Derrick Franklin. Well, guess what, Mr. Franklin? The Music City is going to put you out of your misery. You're not going to come up here and kill for the thrill of it, and have the audacity, and the arrogance, to believe that you're going to walk free and clear. Not on my watch!"

After he was done, Rutherford stepped aside, as Metro Spokesman, John Barron stepped up to the podium, cleared his throat, and began to claim his moment in the spotlight, which was initially created by D-Mac.

"I share the same sentiments as Mr. Rutherford. It's time that we begin making true examples of outsiders who come into our city, bringing violent and deadly criminal acts with them. The violence being committed in our communities by outsiders must stop, and it must stop *NOW*!

"Since his arrival in Nashville, Derrick Franklin has murdered, in cold blood, not one, not two, but four individuals whom we are currently aware of. On Saturday, he murdered Kevin Gilmore and DeVonté Madison; then, on Tuesday, he murdered his own wife, Rayne Morgan-Franklin, and a prominent private investigator, Justin Morris.

"As Mr. Rutherford stated earlier, the filing of this Federal lawsuit, is just a ploy to avoid receiving a life sentence or worse. Derrick Franklin does not deserve to be roaming our streets. He is an extremely dangerous individual, and a cold-blooded murderer. How a Judge could possess the gall to give him *any* type of bond, especially one set so low as $100,000 is beyond me.

"Plus, the fact that a Federal Judge is actually giving this lowlife's Complaint; Motion and Request some sincere consideration, instead of dismissing it all on the spot, actually goes to show that our judicial system is going to hell in a hand basket. May God have mercy on us all."

"Wow!" D-Mac and Shannon exclaimed, almost simultaneously.

"They just gave Judge Lawrence about six minutes' worth of reasons to grant my TRO and Request for Preliminary Injunction." D-Mac stated.

"I can't believe they just went on National television and ranted the way they just did!" Shannon exclaimed. "Are they really *that* stupid?"

"It appears to me that both of 'em just embarked on a joint-venture down a path of self-destruction." D-Mac responded. "And you know what!"

"What?"

"I'm gonna help 'em crash and burn!"

"Finish getting ready. I'm going to call Letha and Jennifer, to see if they saw what we just saw."

RETRIBUTION&REVENGE**RETRIBUTION&REVENGE**RETRIBUTION&REVENGE

D-Mac, Shannon, Letha and Jennifer arrived at the United States Courthouse on Broadway, at a quarter to nine. They walked past the crowd of reporters shouting questions and asking if the quartet had any comments to the earlier press conference. They kept walking and acted as though they weren't even there.

They went through the normal routine as the Judge entered the courtroom, and took his seat behind the bench.

"We're here today to conduct hearings regarding a Request for Temporary Restraining Order and a Request for Preliminary Injunction, in the case of Derrick Franklin versus Jason Rutherford; John Barron; the City of Nashville; and the State of Tennessee.

"Before we begin, I would like to express my genuine thoughts towards the tasteless press conference held in front of this Courthouse moments ago, by Defendants Rutherford and Barron. The two of you are supposed to be public officials. Professionals. You want to degrade Mr. Franklin and call him a 'lowlife,' but during his press conference yesterday, he displayed more professionalism, integrity and dignity than the both of you combined.

Then, not only do you insult the Judge who gave him bail, which is a right afforded to Mr. Franklin by the United States Constitution, but you also had the nerve to insult me, just moments before walking into my courtroom. Then, to make matters worse, you degraded the entire judicial system.

"Before I proceed, I'll state for the record that Mr. Franklin's Request for Temporary Restraining Order, as it pertains to Mr., Rutherford and Mr. Barron, is hereby granted. Also, if Mr. Franklin doesn't convince me to grant his Request for Preliminary Injunction, I will lodge a Complaint myself, with the Board of Professional Responsibility regarding you, Mr. Rutherford. I'll also lodge a Complaint regarding you, Mr. Barron, with the Fraternal Order of Police. You probably already suspect this, but I'm willing to assume that Mr. Franklin will do the same. You may begin when you're ready, Mr. Franklin."

"Thank you, Your Honor." D-Mac responded, as he stood up. "In *Winter v. Natural Residential Defense Council, Incorporated*, 2008, the United States Supreme Court held that a plaintiff seeking preliminary injunction must establish that he is likely to succeed on the merits, that he is likely to suffer irreparable harm in the absence of preliminary relief, that the balance of the equities tip in his favor, and that an injunction is in the public interest."

"I'm sorry Your Honor." Samuel Rutledge interrupted. "This injunction should be denied, due to the fact that granting said injunction would dispose of the case without a trial, which the Defendants are entitled to."

"Mr. Rutledge," Judge Lawrence interjected. "The preliminary injunction is only requesting that they both be suspended without pay, pending disposition. In his prayer for relief, he's requesting termination of their employment, and punitive damages in the neighborhood of seven figures."

"I understand that Your Honor. However, in *Dunn v. Retail Clerks International*, 1962, the Sixth Circuit of the U.S. Court of Appeals declined to issue an injunction pending appeal, after the district court denied the application for a mandatory injunction and dismissed the case."

"Your Honor…" D-Mac began.

"Hold on Mr. Franklin," Judge Lawrence interrupted. "Mr. Rutledge, I'll tell you what I'm going to do. I'm going to do everyone a favor right this moment. Mr. Franklin, your request for preliminary injunction is hereby granted, with the added stipulation that a gag order be levied upon both Mr. Rutherford and Mr. Barron, effectively immediately."

"Your Honor, I'd like to request, ver batim, that you alter or amend that judgment." Rutledge argued.

"Motion denied."

"Now, I'm asking that you reconsider the denial of that motion!"

"Again, denied."

"You're a disgrace to the bench!" Rutledge shouted.

Judge Lawrence rapped his gavel.

"You're in contempt Mr. Rutledge!"

"You ought to hold yourself in contempt!"

"That's twice, Mr. Rutledge!" Judge Lawrence said, as he rapped his gavel repeatedly. "I hereby charge you with Contempt in violation of 18 U.S.C. section 401. You are hereby ordered to spend ninety days in detention and sanctioned a fine in the amount of $1,000! Deputy, remove this man from my courtroom!"

"Your Honor," D-Mac proceeded cautiously. "Would it be too soon to request Summary Judgment, pursuant to Rule 56 of the Federal Rules of Civil Procedure?"

"Mr. Franklin," Judge Lawrence responded. "File your motion with this Court, in writing, accompanied by a Memorandum in Support, and we'll go from there."

"Thank you, Your Honor."

"This Court is adjourned."

RETRIBUTION&REVENGE**RETRIBUTION&REVENGE**RETRIBUTION&REVENGE

"Damn! I didn't expect that." D-Mac stated.

"Neither did I." Letha agreed.

They stopped at the podium, which had been used by Rutherford and Barron earlier that morning.

"As of fifteen minutes ago," D-Mac began. "Assistant District Attorney, Jason Rutherford, and Metro Police Spokesman, John Barron, have both been suspended without pay, pending the disposition of this case, pursuant to Federal Court Order. They have also been placed under a gag order by Judge Lawrence, so there won't be any more outlandish temper tantrums, disguised as press conferences from them.

"Also, District Attorney, Samuel Rutledge, was charged with two consecutive counts of Contempt for disruptive comments he made to Judge Lawrence, after he granted my request for preliminary injunction. He was immediately sentenced to serve ninety days in detention, and ordered to pay a $1,000 fine. Contrary to what Rutherford and Barron said earlier, the judicial system does work. Thank you all for your time."

With that being said, D-Mac ended the press conference and he, along with his defense team, left the United States Courthouse.

Letha and Jennifer returned to their hotel rooms, but D-Mac and Shannon decided to make a stop at the Davidson County District Attorney's Office.

RETRIBUTION&REVENGERETRIBUTION&REVENGE**RETRIBUTION&REVENGE**

"How may I help you?" the young, yet pleasant secretary asked, as they approached her desk.

"I'm trying to figure out which A.D.A. is assigned to my case, because I need to find out when my preliminary hearing is scheduled for." D-Mac responded.

"And your name?"

"Derrick G. Franklin."

"It says here that Jason Rutherford is assigned to your case." She said, after entering his name into the database.

"So, my case hasn't been reassigned yet." He said, more a statement than a question.

"No. Why would it be?" she asked, obviously puzzled.

"So, you haven't heard?"

"Heard what?"

"Jason Rutherford been suspended without pay, pending the outcome of a Federal Civil Rights Complaint, and Samuel Rutledge is servin' three months in federal detention for contempt." D-Mac explained. "I'm surprised you didn't know, seein' as how it has been covered by CNN, *Good Morning America* and tha *Today Show*."

"Wow!" she exclaimed.

"Yeah." D-Mac chuckled. "I thought tha same thing when I was getting calls that it was televised live on CNN."

"Wait a minute." She began. "You're the one they were talking about?"

"I'm tha one!"

She turned, grabbed the phone, and placed a call.

"Sharon, you need to get up here, like, now!" she said, before hanging up the phone. "You wouldn't mind waiting for a minute, would you?"

"I guess not." D-Mac answered.

After a few minutes had passed, a middle-aged woman walked hurriedly through the door.

"What's so important?" she asked.

It became obvious that this was Sharon.

"Your time has arrived!" the secretary told her. "You are finally in charge of the Davidson County District Attorney's Office!"

"Stop playing!" Sharon retorted.

"No, seriously!"

"But how?"

The secretary pointed at D-Mac and stated: "Your Guardian Angel!"

After D-Mac offered a play-by-play account of what occurred in Federal Court that morning, Sharon was obviously stunned.

"So, let me get this straight." She attempted to reason. "Not only did you get the A.D.A. of your case temporarily canned, but also got the head D.A. incarcerated on Federal Contempt charges?"

"Wait a minute!" D-Mac said, holding his hands up, in mock surrender. "I can only take credit for getting Rutherford sidelined. As for Rutledge, he did dat on his own!"

"I still can't believe that I'm now in charge!" she said smiling.

"Well, now that it's been established that you're now in charge," D-Mac began. "I was wondering if you could do me a slight favor."

"Let me guess. Dismiss the charges against you?"

"No! Of course not!" he responded. "That'll make people doubt if you're capable of handling such a job responsibly."

"True." She agreed. "So, what *do* you want?"

"Could you go ahead and assign another A.D.A. to tha case and have them to ask the Judge to schedule a preliminary hearing as soon as he possibly can?"

"Now *that*, I can do." She smiled.

"Thank you!" D-Mac said, as he handed her his number. "Gimme a call and let me know who you assigned and tha date of tha preliminary hearing."

"You're welcome." She responded. "And I'll get that information to you as soon as I can!"

After that exchange, D-Mac and Shannon returned to her house, where they discussed the possibilities and different arguments they could pursue in the hearing.

RETRIBUTION&REVENGE**RETRIBUTION&REVENGE**RETRIBUTION&REVENGE

The following morning, the Interim District Attorney for Davidson County, called D-Mac and notified him that the new Assistant District Attorney was Stanley Wilcox, who had been with the Office a little over eighteen months. She also told him that his preliminary hearing was set for Tuesday, the 26th day of May. He still had a month and a half to prepare.

Saturday, April 18, 2009

D-Mac was up, showered and dressed by five o'clock. Since he was notified that his preliminary hearing was a month and a half away, he had to return to Memphis and take care of a few issues, which couldn't wait.

Shannon agreed to accompany him, and Letha and Jennifer followed, so that they could take care of a few affairs as well. They would have to stay a couple of weeks, seeing as how they had to deal with several cases before returning to Nashville to assist D-Mac with his defense. It would also prove to be *the* biggest case of their careers, seeing as how it was being covered nationally.

When they arrived in Memphis, they exited I-40 West at Highland Avenue. They stopped at the Exxon TigerMarket, at the intersection of Poplar and highland Avenues, for gas. After filling their tanks and saying their goodbyes, Letha and Jennifer went their way, while D-Mac headed to his home on Boxwood Green Lane.

"Wow!" Shannon whispered. "*This* is *your* house?"

"Yeah." He smiled. "It's not much, but it's home."

"Not much?! How many bedrooms do you have?"

"It has four bedrooms, three and a half baths, a gourmet kitchen with island and granite counters, a living room and a two-car garage, among other things."

"It had to run you a mill easy."

"Nah! Just a light $650,000." He responded, as they both exited the car.

"$650,000?!" she asked in disbelief.

"Yeah."

"If you call that light, then I might need to up my rate on you." She joked.

He gave her a guided tour of the house. He could tell that she was impressed. It was a mansion compared to her four-bedroom, three bath home.

"Wait a minute." She said, as they entered the garage. "You have two Acuras *and* two Lexus?"

"Actually," he explained. "I only have one and one. I bought tha otha two for Rayne, but since she no longer needs 'em, I was thankin' 'bout sellin' 'em."

"What do you want for them?" she asked.

"I don't know yet. Why? You want 'em?"

"I wouldn't mind buying the Lexus from you."

"How 'bout this." He reasoned. "Why don't I give you tha Lexus, and that'll make us even for your legal services?"

"Under two conditions."

"Name 'em."

"I still get tha added assistance *and* the sex!"

"Deal!" he agreed, as he kissed her.

After packing all of his clothing in garment and luggage bags, he loaded them in the trunks and back seats of both Lexus vehicles.

He then sat at the computer in a bedroom, which he had converted into a home office, and began preparing advertisements listing the sale of both Acura vehicles, and placing the house on the market for rent. He wanted nothing that would remind him of Rayne.

The listing for the house read:

> **EAST**, Boxwood Green Lane, 4BR/3.5BA, lg. gourmet kit. w/ granite counters; LR w/ FP & 12' ceiling; 2-car gar.; fenced bkyd; stainless steel app.; W/D; fully furn. inc'g six 62" plasmas. $2500 dep. + $2000/mo. Ready to move in! 901-555-2274. Ask for "D". Ser. Inq. Only!

The listing for the Acuras read:

> **ACURAs, 2009**, matching TSX sedans; titanium grey w/ grey lthr; P/DL; P/W; P/Seats; P/Steering; ABS; RKE; custom snd syst.; 1 owner; gar. kpt; under fact. warr.; one has 22" chrm wheels; 1200 mi; asking $34K. The other has 20" chrm wheel; 300 mi; asking $33K. Ser. Inq. only! 901-555-2274. Ask for "D".

When he was done, D-Mac asked Shannon for her opinion, before he submitted them.

"They're actually pretty good and quite thorough." She remarked.

"That's what I was aimin' for." He said, as he submitted them online. "Now, all I have to do is wait."

"What are you going to do with her clothes?"

"I told her parents that I'll send all her personal belongings to them."

"When's the funeral?"

"Don't know and don't care."

"Wouldn't it look odd if you didn't at least show up?"

"I told her parents I was too distraught to attend."

"You need to go!" she nearly demanded. "If you don't, it'll only fan the rumors and speculations that you were involved. If it'll help, I'll go with you."

"Wouldn't *that* be odd, to show up at my wife's funeral with another woman on my arm?"

"Everyone who's been following the situation knows that I'm lead counsel of your defense team." She reasoned. "I'm sure Letha and Jennifer wouldn't mind coming along as well."

"Fuck it. Why not?" he sighed, as he picked up the phone. "Might as well."

He called Rayne's parents and obtained the details of Rayne's service. It was scheduled to take place on Tuesday, the 21st of April. He really didn't want to go, but Shannon was right. It would seem odd if he didn't go.

D-Mac spent the rest of Saturday and most of Sunday, showing Shannon around Memphis. They had a good time, and Shannon really enjoyed herself. Sunday evening, they headed back to Nashville. D-Mac in his Lexus LS460, and Shannon in her relatively new Lexus ISF.

Tuesday, April 24, 2009

    D-Mac entered the small church, dressed in a black, denim set; black shirt; black shoes; and black sunglasses. He was followed closely by Shannon, who was behind him, with Letha and Jennifer on either side of him. The three of them wore black dresses and sunglasses also.

    They ushered him down the center aisle of the packed church, to Rayne's casket, as everyone in attendance watched. D-Mac reached down and touched her hand, which was, of course, ice cold and hard as a brick. Everyone watched as he leaned down to whisper something into her ear.

"I loved you. I really did." He barely whispered. "But you lied to me. I would've let you live, but you made tha fatal mistake of tryna snitch me out. Good riddance, you rat."

He stood up as Shannon; Letha and Jennifer led him to a section cleared for the four of them on the front row. As they sat down, they were approached by an older white man, whom they assumed was Rayne's father.

"She talked about you constantly whenever she called." He said, as he knelt in front of D-Mac. "She truly loved you, and I believe that you truly loved her, too."

"I did." D-Mac interrupted. "She tha one who convinced me to go completely legit. I promise you Mr. Morgan, if it's ever discovered who did this, I'll kill 'em dead. They might try to give me tha death penalty for doin' so, but it'll be for a good reason."

Rayne's father looked at D-Mac for a moment, then went back to join his wife.

"What did he say?" Mrs. Morgan asked her husband, when he returned to her side.

"He promised that if it's discovered who killed Rayne, he'll kill them himself."

"Do you think he was involved?"

"I seriously doubt it." He answered. "If he did, then he's a damned good actor."

The service lasted two hours, after which they attended the interment at the cemetery. Even though he really didn't want to, Shannon and Letha convinced D-Mac to attend the gathering at Rayne's parents' home, which followed the grave-side service.

RETRIBUTION&REVENGE**RETRIBUTION&REVENGE**RETRIBUTION&REVENGE

After Rayne's parents introduced D-Mac and his legal team to the rest of the family, they sat around and told D-Mac of their fondest memories of Rayne. Recollections which he knew would have embarrassed her, had she been there.

After an hour of this, D-Mac stood and thanked everyone for their hospitality.

"Do you have to go?" her mother asked.

"Unfortunately, I do." He responded. "We have a lotta preppin' to do for my preliminary hearing that's comin' up. Plus, I gotta keep my ear to tha streets if I wanna find tha bastards that killed Rayne before tha police do."

"Listen to me man." A cousin, who was introduced to D-Mac as Bruce, tried to reason. "She wouldn't want you to do that. If anything, she'd want you to let the justice system do what it's supposed to do."

"First of all, tha justice system is a joke. It got me fightin' two first-degree murda charges, which I didn't do." He began. "My record speaks for itself. If I did it with good reason, I'll take it to trial and put up a defense for a lesser included conviction."

"C'mon. Let's go." Letha told him, trying to calm him down.

"No! I'm not done!' he nearly yelled. "I don't know how y'all do thangs down here in Clifton, but in Memphis, retaliation is a must! Not sometimes; not maybe; but it's mandatory! Rayne knew who and how I am! She knew about my Gangsta ways, and she knew how I get down! So, excuse me if I don't agree with your forgive and forget mumbo jumbo!

"When someone I care about and love gets murdered in cold-blood, I seek and receive revenge. When I find 'em, they betta make they peace with God, because I'ma personally make sho' they get a one-way ticket to meet Him!"

"D-Mac! Stop!" Letha yelled. "That's enough! Let's go!"

"How'd I do?" D-Mac asked, as they pulled off the property.

"They looked like they didn't know whether to run or hug you." Letha said.

"Hell, you had me convinced!" Shannon added.

"I know one thing." Jennifer commented.

"What's that?" D-Mac asked.

"All y'all krazie as hell!" she laughed.

They pretty much rode in silence, all the way back to Nashville.

Tuesday, May 26, 2009

The day D-Mac had been preparing for was finally at hand. The preliminary hearing was set to begin at nine o'clock that morning. D-Mac had made a point to do thorough research on his opponent, who, even though he was a rookie in the District Attorney's Office, he wanted to know everything he could find on him.

Stanley Wilcox was thirty-four years old, and was originally from Texas. He was a graduate of both Vanderbilt University Law School and Harvard Law. After finishing at Harvard, he decided to return to Nashville. After interning at a couple of law firms in

Nashville, he applied for and received a job as an Assistant District Attorney, for Davidson County.

His mother was till in Texas, and his father had been killed in combat, while serving in Desert Storm. He has two older sisters, both of whom are doctors, and a younger brother, who had just graduated high school, and wanted to follow in his brother's footsteps.

In his twenty-one-month career with the D.A.'s Office, his record currently stood at four wins; two losses; six mistrials or hung juries; and over twenty-five plea bargains. He was ecstatic when his new boss, Sharon Rogers, assigned him to D-Mac's double homicide case.

As soon as he was assigned, he called his family back home and told them that he had been assigned to the high-profile, double homicide in Nashville, where the original A.D.A. had been suspended without pay, and the District Attorney himself had been charged with Federal Contempt charges, and sentenced to three months' imprisonment. He told them that the entire trial would more than likely be televised on CNN, and that this would be his chance to make a name for himself.

His mother expressed her concerns about him getting his hopes up so high, but he told her that the Defendant was basically representing himself, bit had three female attorneys to assist him. He assured her that this trial would be as simple as taking candy from a baby. But, little did he realize, the baby he was referring to, had a lot of knowledge to fight with.

RETRIBUTION&REVENGERETRIBUTION&REVENGE**RETRIBUTION&REVENGE**

After the Judge had entered the Courtroom and everyone had been seated, he commenced the preliminary hearing.

"We're here to conduct a preliminary hearing in the case of State v. Franklin, case number 2009-B-348." Judge Isaiah Howard began. "Mr. Franklin, you're being charged with two counts of First-Degree Murder; one count of Unlawful Possession of a Firearm by a Convicted Felon; one count of Unlawful Possession of a Firearm with Felony Intent; and one count of Felony Reckless Endangerment. How do you plead?"

"Not guilty on all counts, Your Honor." D-Mac responded.

"You may present your case Mr. Wilcox."

"Thank you, sir." Stanley Wilcox began. "The State intends to prove that Derrick G. Franklin, committed the premeditated First-Degree Murders of both Kevin Gilmore and DeVonté Madison, on April 11th. In doing so, the State will also prove that Mr. Franklin is guilty of being a convicted felon in possession of a firearm, and that he unlawfully possessed a firearm with felony intent. Furthermore, due to the fact that there were numerous individuals in the vicinity at the time he committed these gruesome murders, he's also guilty of Felony Reckless Endangerment."

"Mr. Franklin?" the Judge began. "I understand that you have chosen to represent yourself, but has retained counsel to assist you. Is that correct?"

"It is Your Honor."

"You may proceed."

"Thank you. Mr. Wilcox sounds quite convincing!" D-Mac stated, sarcastically. "I'm almost certain that the spectators here today, may sense that the State has a well-grounded case. The fact, however, is that they don't. Their entire case is barely circumstantial, at best.

"I'm curious to know how Mr. Wilcox plans to prove these theories when, for one, out of roughly a dozen witness statements, no two witness statements can corroborate one another as to the identity of the suspected gunman. None of the alleged eyewitness statements given, accurately described or identified me as the shooter; none of them identified my vehicle as the alleged 'getaway' vehicle; none of them gave corroborating descriptions as to the weapons allegedly used; and none of them produced a full or even accurate partial description of my plates.

"The State claims to be able to prove that I possessed a firearm with felony intent, and while being a convicted felon. How? How can they prove such, when the murder weapon hasn't been located? They have no forensic evidence; no fingerprints; and no ballistic reports, which can positively identify me as the shooter."

D-Mac returned to the defense table ad retrieved two documents, handing one to A.D.A. Wilcox, and the other to the Judge.

"I shall, at this time, move this Honorable Court to suppress the photo identification utilized by the Metro Police Department, pursuant to…"

"Objection!" Wilcox shouted, as he jumped up from his seat. "There's nothing wrong with the photo line-up!"

"Your Honor," D-Mac proceeded. "If I may, can I present my reasons for asking for suppression?"

"Your objection is overruled." The Judge rendered. "You may proceed."

"Thank you. In *Simmons v. United States*, decided in 1968, the United States Supreme Court held that an identification procedure that is so impermissibly suggestive, as to give rise to a very substantial likelihood of irreparable misidentification, violates due process."

"So, how was the identification procedure suggestive?" Judge Howard asked.

"Because the photographic array used in the procedure, which contained six photographs, was extremely prejudicial."

"How so?"

"Out of six photographs, five were of inmates in orange jumpsuits, associated with the Davidson County Sheriff's Office. The sixth photo, however, was the photograph taken when I was booked into the Shelby County Jail, which uses dark blue shirts and pants for the inmate attire. So, of course, your witnesses are going to be drawn to that photograph."

"I see." Replied Judge Howard. "Mr. Wilcox. Do you have any witnesses here you'd like to call, before I rule on Mr. Franklin's Motion to Suppress?"

"Yes, Your Honor. I'd like to first call Tony Matthews."

After he was sworn in, A.D.A. Wilcox began his direct examination.

"Mr. Matthews, do you recall the events which occurred in the University Court housing projects on Saturday, April 11th of this year?"

"Yes sir."

"Would you describe what you remember to the Court?"

"Sure." He responded. "I was sittin' on tha porch with a coupla friends, when we heard a buncha shootin'. When it stopped, we saw dude jump in a tan car and peel out."

"Peel out?" Wilcox asked.

"Yeah. His tires was spinnin' and screamin' when he took off."

"Oh. I gotcha. Do you see tha individual who jumped in the tan car and drove off in the courtroom today?"

"Yeah."

"Will you point him out for the Court?"

The witness pointed at D-Mac.

"Let the record reflect that the witness has identified the defendant, Mr. Franklin." Wilcox requested.

"It has been noted." Judge Howard stated.

"Thank you. No Further question."

"Mr. Franklin, would you like to cross?"

"It's be my pleasure," D-Mac smiled, as he stood up. "Mr. Matthews. When you heard the shooting begin, what was your initial reaction?"

"Me and my friends was tryna take cover, 'cause we didn't know where tha shootin' was comin' from at first."

"So, where did you end up taking cover at?"

"When we first heard tha shootin', we ran in tha apartment."

"So, when you hard the first shots, you ran inside, correct?"

"Yeah."

"And when did you go back onto the porch, or when did you go back outside?"

"Not long after tha shootin' stopped."

"What is 'not long'?"

"I don't know." He responded nervously. "A coupla minutes, maybe?"

"A couple of minutes?"

"Yeah."

"So, you're telling this Court that I allegedly shot and killed two individuals, then waited a 'couple of minutes,' as you say, before I got in my car and drove off?"

"Yeah."

"Okay. Let's say, hypothetically speaking, that you're telling the truth." D-Mac suggested. "How many individuals did you see in the car?"

"Just one."

"So, I was alone?"

"Yes."

"Would you consider yourself a car guy?"

"Objection! Relevance?!" Wilcox shouted.

"I'm leading up to the relevant question." D-Mac stated.

"Overruled."

"Now, Mr. Matthews," D-Mac continued. "Would you consider yourself a car guy?"

"What you mean?"

"I mean, would you be able to tell the make and model of a car by cursory glance?"

"Oh, yeah!"

"Okay. So, what was the make and model of the car I was driving, on the day of the shooting?"

"It was a tan-colored Toyota Camry."

"Did it have tints on the windows?"

"Not that I can remember."

"Could we dim the lights, please?" D-Mac requested.

He walked over to his laptop, and after hitting a few keys, a photograph appeared on a screen.

"So, this is the car that you saw me drive off in?"

"Yes."

"Let the record reflect that the witness is referring to a 2007 Toyota Camry, tan in color."

"It has been noted." Judge Howard confirmed.

After D-Mac pressed a few more keys, another photograph appeared.

"Do you know the make and model of this vehicle?"

"It's a Lexus LS."

Once again, D-Mac hit a couple of keys, to produce yet another image.

"Can you see what that is?" D-Mac asked.

"It look like a car title."

"Can you tell us the name of the owner on the title?"

"Derrick Franklin." He answered, nervously.

"Now, can you tell us the year, make, model and color of the vehicle this title belongs to?"

"A 2009 Lexus LS460L, champagne-colored."

"Now," D-Mac said, as he hit another key on his laptop. "Do you recognize this vehicle?"

"It's tha same Lexus you showed before."

"Yes and no."

"I don't understand."

"The first Lexus I showed you was from an advertisement listing the vehicle for sale. This Lexus is the one that I own, which is described on the title I just showed."

"Okay."

"Now, in your earlier testimony, you stated that I was alone in the vehicle. Is that correct?"

"Yes."

"As you can see from this photo, My Lexus has five percent window tinting, which is also called 'limo tinting.' So, how could you possibly tell whether I was alone or not?"

"I couldn't."

"So, you not only gave a false statement to the police investigators, but you just lied to this Court. Am I right?"

"Naw man!"

"So, you didn't just lie to this Court, while under oath?" D-Mac nearly shouted.

"Objection! He's badgering the witness!" Wilcox yelled.

"Your Honor. Will you *please* instruct the witness to answer the question posed to him?" D-Mac asked, more calmly.

"Your objection is overruled. Mr. Matthews, answer the question. Did you, or did you not, just perjure yourself?"

"I was just doin' what they told me!"

"What *who* told you?" Judge Howard demanded, as he glowered down at the witness stand.

"Mr. Rutherford." He replied. "He told me to pick Derrick franklin outta tha lineup, or he was gonna charge me with obstructin' or somethin'."

"Your Honor…" D-Mac began.

"You don't have to say it Mr. Franklin." Judge Howard interrupted. "Based on what I just heard from this witness, it's apparent that this entire case has been tainted by A.D.A. Rutherford."

"Wait a minute, Your Honor," Wilcox interrupted. "I'll agree with you on suppressing the phot lineup, but you *cannot* seriously be considering dismissing the entire case!"

"From the evidence that I've seen, which is next to nothing, you have no case Mr. Wilcox. The shell casings recovered at the scene yielded no fingerprints; the police have yet to locate the murder weapon or weapons; the photographic array used in the lineup was *highly* suggestive and is *very* prejudicial to Mr. Franklin.

"If that's not bad enough, the individual who is listed as the State's *star* witness, was just decimated by Mr. Franklin during *preliminary*, during which, this same *star* witness admitted that he perjured himself, at the direction of, and under duress by A.D.A. Rutherford.

"Now, if you still wish to proceed with the prosecution of this case, while making a mockery of the law, I suggest that you locate another Judge to assist you in that endeavor, as I refuse to allow you to use *my* courtroom to grandstand in front of the media.

"I understand your position. Believe me, I do. You're relatively new to the Davidson County D.A.'s Office; you've been assigned to a case that haws unexpectedly become a high-profile case, attracting national media coverage; and your Defendant, representing himself, has embarrassed you, beat you senseless, and is sending you home with you tail tucked between your legs.

"Mr. Franklin," Judge Howard continued. "Congratulations on your victory. I'm granting your obvious Motion for Judgment of Acquittal. This case is hereby dismissed, with prejudice, and you're free to go. I will, however, say this. I honestly don't know whether you were the shooter in this case. But, if you were, then I hope the souls of both victims torture and torment you in your dreams for the remainder of your life. I don't ever want to see you in my courtroom again. Do you understand?"

"Yes, Your Honor." D-Mac responded. "And for the record, I wasn't the shooter, and I don't appreciate the statement you made about me being tortured and tormented.

"Given the circumstances, however, I'll grant you a pass. Otherwise, I wouldn't hesitate to embarrass you in federal court as I did D.A. Rutledge and A.D.A. Rutherford. Thank you for the acquittal, and have a wonderful day."

D-Mac then turned and left the courtroom, followed by Shannon, Letha and Jennifer. When they left the Courthouse, they approached the bank of microphones, which had been set up on the courthouse steps.

"Once again, lies were demolished; the truth brought to light, and corruption revealed. The system may not always be right, and innocent Defendants pay the price. Fortunately for me, the system acted according to law, and justice has prevailed. Thank you!"

They all watched as D-Mac and his Defense team, crossed the street and climbed in the Lexus, which was the focal point of his argument and presentation, which ultimately led to the Judgment of Acquittal in his favor.

RETRIBUTION&REVENGE**RETRIBUTION&REVENGE**RETRIBUTION&REVENGE

"Do you think they'll try to recharge him?" Jennifer asked, as they ate a celebratory dinner at Shannon's house.

"They can't." Shannon responded. "A Judgment of Acquittal is the same as a not guilty verdict handed down by a jury. Therefore, double jeopardy is attached."

"You got lucky on that one." Jennifer told him.

"Not really." D-Mac responded.

"What you mean 'not really'?" Letha asked.

"Hell, I did time at Whiteville with Tony, back in like, 2004."

"Wait a minute." Letha said, as she tried to comprehend the meaning of the revelation D-Mac had just revealed. "You mean that you set that shit up from the jump?"

"Yeah. When we was in tha apartment, I called and told him what was up, and he said to do what I had to do, and that he had my back."

"So, what about the other witnesses?" Shannon asked.

"They all from U.C., which is where Tony was raised." D-Mac explained. "All tha witnesses who came forward, did so 'cause he told 'em to, only after tellin' 'em what to report to tha police."

"You a mess with yourself!" Shannon teased. "You know that, right?"

"Hey! I wouldn't be me if I wasn't!" he said, causing everyone to laugh.

EPILOGUE

In the weeks following the Court's granting of his Motion for Judgment of Acquittal, D-Mac's life changed dramatically, along with the lives of those close to him. Despite the recent turn of events, the changes experienced by everyone were all positive.

D-Mac finally began the permanent transition of settling into Shannon's four-bedroom; three bath home on Lischey Avenue in East Nashville. In addition to D-Mac, Letha and Jennifer also decided to relocate to Nashville.

They both chipped in on a four-bedroom; three bath home, located at 2157 Christina Court, for an affordable $250,000 price tag. It even included an office, which they decided would be especially useful. Their homes in Memphis were placed on the market for rent, and they meticulously scrutinized a carefully selected group of individuals within their Memphis firm, before choosing the one who would take the reigns as office manager. They also let it be known that they would drop in, periodically and unannounced, to make sure that everything was running smoothly.

D-Mac filed for, and was granted Summary Judgment in his Federal lawsuit. Instead of the $10 Million he was initially demanding in the original complaint, an agreement was reached for the substantial amount of $4.5 Million, with $1.5 Million to be paid up front. The remaining $3 Million would be paid in annual installments of $100,000.

He bought a 2192 square-foot commercial building for $250,000 cash, located at 1200 Clay Street. It was here, that he opened *Franklin's Paralegal Group*. In the same building, Letha and Jennifer opened the Nashville branch of their firm, which included Shannon as a partner.

Two authors approached D-Mac, proposing to write a book about his recent legal issues. He declined both offers, and instead, opted to write and self-publish a book himself. He, along with his now famous legal team, agreed to conduct interviews with multiple CNN anchors; the *Today Show*; *Good Morning America*; *60 Minutes*; *20/20* and *Dateline*. They were surprised by, and accepted, an invitation to BET's *106 & Park*.

D-Mac also agreed, after strenuous negotiations, to participate in documentaries created and filmed by CourtTV; the History Channel; the Discovery Channel; Lifetime; and A&E. He agreed to speak with high school students regarding his struggles coming up in Memphis; his time in prison; receiving his Paralegal Certification; and his recent trial.

Two years after the commencement of the Nashville fiasco, D-Mac received national coverage again, when he received a full pardon by Tennessee's Governor. A few months later, he accepted an invitation to the White House.

After six years, following the double homicide in Nashville, the spotlight began to fade. D-Mac called a meeting with his legal team, consisting of Letha; Jennifer and Shannon. It was then, that he told them of a second book he had written, and had been sitting on. It was a major bombshell, which he had meticulously created, and now was the time to detonate it.

It was the true account of what had taken place in University Court on Saturday, April 11, 2009, surrounding the double homicide. Since double jeopardy had been attached, thanks to the Judgment of Acquittal, and his record had been wiped clean with a governor's pardon, there was nothing anyone could do about it. The written confession was sure to be a national best seller, with an appropriate title: *"Intelligent Sociopath: How I Got Away with Premeditated Murder."*

Made in the USA
Columbia, SC
08 August 2021